Eddystone Light

A Novella

Amelia Smith

Eddystone Light: A Novella

ISBN: 1941334024
ISBN-13: 978-1-941334-02-7

Print edition February 2014

Cover Design by Amelia Smith and Michael Craughwell

http://www.ameliasmith.net

TABLE OF CONTENTS

Chapter One: On the Rocks..p. 1

Chapter Two: Journeys Ashore..p. 13

Chapter Three: Carnival Men...p. 31

Chapter Four: Engagements..p. 55

Chapter Five: Jack at Sea..p. 83

The Song Behind the Story ....p. 101

CHAPTER ONE: ON THE ROCKS

August, 1888

Waves washed up to the lighthouse door outside. Jack's father leaned across the hatch-cover table. He poured whiskey into a thick glass and cleared the salt crust from his voice.

"Son," he said, "I want you to marry a land girl. A nice land-girl."

"What do you mean, Father?" Jack straightened his jacket. His town clothes felt out of place here, but they reminded him of his hopes for a respectable life on shore, not a life like his father's, chained to these rocks.

"What I'm saying..." Jack's father braced himself with a shot of whiskey. "I'm saying that you need a girl with two feet who can walk about the place, do your cooking and cleaning, keep you company, nights." Jack ran his hand along table's underside, feeling the barnacles there and wishing he were back on land. His father tapped the last drops from the glass, filled it again to the brim, and passed it to Jack. "That's what you need. Not a mermaid. They never stick around."

"A mermaid? Father!" Jack gathered his breath. He regarded the whiskey with suspicion. He needed to keep his wits about him. Perhaps his father wouldn't notice if he didn't drink. "You should spend some time on shore, Father, if you're seeing mermaids," Jack said.

His father slapped his thigh and rocked back and forth in his chair. "If I'm *seeing* them? No, son, it's *not* seeing them that would drive me back to shore. They hardly ever come around any more, not like when I was a fine young man like you. Not like when I met your mother."

Jack had been raised by his Aunt Ermentrude, in a respectable house in a quiet but unfashionable part of Plymouth. Aunt Ermie had always discouraged questions about his mother.

"Aunt Ermie said that my mother was a woman of ill repute, a trollop, she said once..."

"A scallop?! I never heard of such a thing! Don't be absurd. She might have worn scallops sometimes, but she certainly isn't a scallop."

Jack decided to drink the whiskey after all. He winced at the unaccustomed burn in his throat. "No, she said a trollop. She didn't know I was listening. She was talking to a neighbor."

"Stop right there!" Jack's father shot up out of his seat and pounded the bottle on the table. "That's no way for a woman to talk about her own nephew!"

"Aunt Ermie's all right," Jack said.

The lighthouse keeper shook his head. "I never should have let her have you. Your mother swam here all the way from the coast of Brittany with you in her arms and your brothers beside her. Said she couldn't raise a child with man-legs in the sea."

"I have brothers?"

"I tried to tell her I was no fitter to care for a baby," Jack's father went on, "but she just shimmied her tail and off she swam. What was I to do?" He strode along a worn path across the room as he talked, one finger held aloft, poking at the ceiling overhead, smacking the beams as he passed them, humming. Jack edged his chair closer to the wall.

"It's impossible, irrational," Jack mumbled.

His father heard none of it. "I should come to the point," he said. "Your mother will be here at midnight. She wants to see you."

"What?! Here, in this room?"

"Of course not. Ermie raised you a fool! Don't you know anything about mermaids?"

Jack shrugged. He vaguely remembered his father telling him about mermaids once, but when he'd mentioned the conversation to Aunt Ermie, she'd slapped him and gone off to write a letter to his father. He had been quite small at the time.

"Well, there's something else I want to tell you, before she comes." Jack's father paced to the window and sniffed the air. "If I whisper, she won't hear."

He bent over so that his whiskey-sprinkled beard tickled Jack's ear. "I think she's going to try to marry you off to one of her sea-companions,

3

another mermaid. You mustn't do it."

"'Course I won't," Jack said. As if a mermaid would have him, if mermaids even existed. The girls on land walked across the street when they saw him coming, from respectable young ladies right down to the trollops that Aunt Ermie was always warning him against.

"Swear it to me then!" his father hissed. "Swear it on the landlubber's bible!" He pulled out a green-rusty leather volume and set it on the table. "Swear that you'll marry a land-girl."

"Girls hardly even look my way!" Jack protested.

"But you're a fine cut of a young man! Anyone can see that! I know I'm blinded by a father's love, but you're a fine looking young man!"

Jack blushed. "It's not that. It's the smell." No matter how often Jack bathed, what soaps and scrubs, oils and elixirs he applied, he smelled like a fish, unmistakably like a scaly thing that lived in the sea and had been slightly too long out of water. It repelled females faster than they could be properly introduced.

"Ah, that." Jack's father poured himself another glass of whiskey and sat down. "That's from your mother, I'm afraid. Being half fish and all. Your brothers had more fish in them, much more."

Jack scoured his memories, memories too slippery to keep on hand in the orderly world of Aunt Ermie's household. He remembered a dream of sitting on the rocks outside the lighthouse at low tide, talking to fishes in the shallows. It must have been a dream. He must not get pulled into Father's madness. He remembered two fish in particular who always came to see him, a porpoise and a porgy. Could those be the brothers his father had mentioned? It seemed impossible.

Jack's father turned to the small porthole window and inhaled deeply. "That's her, alright," he said with half a smile. "I can smell her coming." His eye trembled. "You must swear it to me now! Better to be a bachelor than have your heart dragged down to the bottom of the sea!" He startled back at the sound of his own voice. "Too loud, too loud," he whispered to himself. Then he leaned in at Jack again, whispering this time. "Hear me boy, and swear it: If you marry at all, it will be to a land girl. A nice land girl, with two legs, and two good feet."

"All right, father." Jack set his hand on the Bible. "As God is my witness," he began.

"Shh! Quieter! She's coming. She can hear!"

"As God is my witness," Jack whispered, "If I marry it will be to a girl who lives on the land." He removed his hand from the book and looked at his father. "Will that do?"

§

A few hours later, Jack stood on the rocks, looking out across the choppy waves toward France. A light mist hung in the air. His father's lantern shone through one window after the next as he climbed up the lighthouse. Silver moonlight filtered through breaks between the clouds. Phosphorescence glowed in the breaking waves. Everyone knew that mermaids didn't exist. Trollops, while disreputable, were at least well-attested to. Aunt Ermie had always been more reasonable than Father, and Jack aspired to a reasonable life, even if it turned out to be a lonely one. He was going to be an accountant, respectable and secure. He attended the new college in Bristol. Everyone there expected him to do quite well.

Father was clearly becoming un-moored. He and Aunt Ermie ought to reel him back in from the rocks and help set his mind to rights, though perhaps it was already too late. Then again, if Father were right about his brothers, if he had brothers, that would be something. He had always been alone as a child – all the other children had brothers and sisters to play with, companionship, while he only had Aunt Ermie.

Jack started to look for a few mussels for his breakfast. He never minded eating mollusks. They weren't actual fish. They didn't have eyes, or voices. They were more like vegetables. As he leaned down to pull a string of them off a rock, he heard a tinkling, like bells. He shouldn't have had that whiskey. Then a woman's voice called out from starboard.

"Ahoy!"

At first, all Jack could see was a burst of phosphorescence next to a buoy. He squinted.

"I'm dreaming," Jack muttered to himself.

"You most certainly are not!" A fin slapped down, sending up a spray of foam, and she came into focus. Her dark hair, streaked with silver, poured over sea-foam white shoulders, and her breasts bobbed on the waves. As for her eyes, he might have been looking into a mirror. It seemed wrong that she could just swim up here like that.

This was something else again.

"I don't believe we've met," Jack said. "Been properly introduced, I mean. I mean..." He felt his footing falter, and sat down on the rocks. The string of mussels trailed down over his carefully pressed trousers, muddying them. He could hear Aunt Ermie in his head, scolding him about the laundry.

The mermaid swam closer. Sparkling bangles trailed along her arm – they made that bell-like sound. Her tail snaked through the water, covered with iridescent scales. There was no way he could have been born of that, even presuming it were real. "My!" she shook her head. "You do look like a land-dweller. More's the pity." She brushed a tear out of her eye. "And do not start this nonsense about introduction. I hatched you myself, and nursed you at my breast, though it's hard to imagine now. You were my only legged child, and that was so long ago."

Jack stammered. "I... I can't remember a thing. Surely you must realize that?"

"Oh, boys! Such faulty minds," the mermaid sighed.

"But no one can remember their own infancy," Jack protested. "Men of science have proven it."

"Ah, but *we* do," she said. "Our kind do. Try, my son."

So Jack, feeling quite adrift, tried. He closed his eyes and it came to him in waves, along with so much else that he had tried not to remember.

"It's just like a dream, though," Jack said after a while.

"Humph. You might say so now, but you'll learn."

"But you never came back for me," Jack said, "I never saw you, I don't know. Father says you just left me here."

"I *am* your mother, though," she said. "All the rest of my hatchlings were fish, except for Thomas, the porpoise. He was the only other one I nursed, and I consoled myself with him when you had to go to your father. That's why I've come today. Thomas is gone. You are all I have left."

"But where is Georgie? And how can you be my mother?"

"Gone. The fishermen had him last week. He lived a good long life, for a porgy, near sixteen years. It was only you I never heard of." She sniffed, and dabbed her eyes with a piece of ruffly pink seaweed.

"Oh." Jack hung his head. He remembered a jolly fish nibbling at his ankles, making Jack chase him around the rocks. Jack had always been a strong swimmer, but he was no match for that fish.

"As for myself," his mother went on, "I nursed you at my own breast as long as I could keep you warm, but in autumn the water became too cold. You were still so small, floating in the shallows, and Thomas and Georgie needed deeper waters, so I brought you here."

Jack considered. It was not pleasant, to live with the constant shame of being a bastard, but he had gotten used to it. Aunt Ermie had convinced him that his mother was a trollop, a mere doxy, who had heartlessly abandoned him. Having a mermaid mother was preposterous, but perhaps slightly less shameful – even if she were just as heartless as the supposed doxy.

"Mother?" Jack said. "I didn't know you existed, not like this."

The mermaid's eyebrows shot up and her great tail with them. It pounded the sea again, more petulant than a mere stomping of feet. "Like what, son?"

"Like a fish. I suppose I am like a fish too, at least in smell."

"Georgie always smelled dreadfully like a land-dweller."

"It was Thomas and Georgie, wasn't it?" Jack said. "The porpoise and the porgy?" It was as if his memories had been lying on the rocks entangled with the strings of mussels, waiting for him to pick them up again.

"You don't know how dear you are to me, even after all this time apart," his mother said. "I asked after you, but your father never had much to say." She swam closer.

"I'm glad you could come tonight," she said. "I need you to find Thomas."

"Find him?" Jack said, confused. "I... I don't see how I'd be able to help. I mean, he's a porpoise. I haven't seen him in a long time, and I wouldn't know what to look for."

The mermaid slapped her tail on the waves again.

"He is nowhere in the sea!" she cried. "If he can't be found, you will be my only consolation. Don't you see?"

Jack looked at her, wondering again how this could possibly be his mother.

"I could look for him, I suppose," he said slowly. "How long has Tommy been missing?"

"A week," she said. "Not in any corner of the sea, or up the rivers, either. The other porpoises would have heard if he were anywhere that a fish could rightly go. He can only be on the land, if he is anywhere."

"A week isn't so very long," Jack said. "He must be all right. Where was he last seen?"

"Near the mouth of the Thames. Thomas was always going off to London."

"London it is, then," Jack said. He would find his brother, and that would be that. His mother... well, the more he looked at her, the more familiar she became, but she would never be the companion that a brother could be.

"You're such a good boy," his mother sniffed, "such a good boy!"

A band of lighter color grew along the eastern horizon. In the first hints of daylight, the mermaid did look almost old enough to be a mother.

"I must go back to the lighthouse... mother," Jack said. She looked strange and sad, sitting there on the rocks. He stepped into the water and embraced her in the choppy shallows.

She retrieved a barnacle-speckled conch shell from a crevice in the rocks. "Here, take this," she said. "When you come back to the sea, anywhere, blow on it, and I will come. Also, if you meet any fishes in your journey, it will help you talk to them."

The mermaid reached out to embrace Jack once more. "I was so sad to hand you into your father's arms, to be reared by hard land-dwelling strangers," she said. "But now that we've been re-united, you must come back to the sea."

"To the sea? How?" Jack said.

"I ask it as your mother. I can arrange it."

"I've never been one to shirk family obligation," said Jack, "but..."

"We can make you a tail," his mother said. "It will serve quite well. You'll learn to use it in no time, they tell me."

"I don't know about that," Jack said. "I will certainly come visit, though. As I do Father..."

The mermaid pouted. "But I must have a son to keep me company in my old age," she said. "You're the only one I can find!"

Jack thought of coffee, mince pies, and his Aunt Ermentrude, who for all her faults did love him. She had never minded his smell. Coffee and mince pies, those were things he'd never taste again if he had to go live in the sea. He was as sure of it as he was of his own name: Jack the lighthouse keeper's son, or foundling, or the mermaid's son. It didn't matter whose son he was, he wanted mince pies and coffee.

"I will find Thomas, if he's living. I swear it," Jack said, hoping that would allow him a choice, at least. He wasn't in the habit of swearing things, but now he was making an oath for the second time since sundown. The one to his father seemed even more meaningless now. His chances of marrying a girl would go from slim to nothing if he became a merman. The very absurdity of the possibility would have woken him up if he'd been dreaming. What he really wanted, now, was to find his brother. He tried to remember Tommy, smooth grey skin rolling through the surf, telling him all about the sea.

"I will return Thomas to you," Jack said.

"That would be the best of all possible solutions, to reunite our family," the mermaid said, "but if you would return to the sea, too... You're such a clever young man. You'll remember." Jack's mother kissed his forehead, sniffling back her tears, which were so salty that they almost crystallized as they rolled down her cheeks. "Go then. Find him."

With that, Jack's mermaid mother turned her shimmering tail and dove into the dawn-dusted sea.

§

CHAPTER TWO: JOURNEYS ASHORE

G od go with you, my boy," the lighthouse-keeper said, helping him into the rowboat. The smugglers didn't like his town clothes and respectable aspirations. If they knew who, or what, his mother was, they would probably throw him overboard, despite his father.

"Keep safe, father," Jack said. "Aunt Ermie says you can come stay with her any time." It wasn't strictly true, but she wouldn't turn him away.

"No, no, son. Off you go." He pulled Jack close and whispered in his ear. "Remember: a nice land girl. That's the most important thing."

Jack nodded, but it wasn't the most important thing to him, not any more. He settled into the front of the gig, opposite the pilot, and waved to his father as they pulled away. The oarsmen leaned into their work, sparing little breath for talk. The sooner they reached shore, the sooner they'd all get their drams of whiskey and a share of the night's profits.

As they rowed, Jack remembered Georgie talking about life in the sea, and Thomas asking what it was like on land. Jack would have swum with them all night, but father called him back to the rocks at supper time. His brothers were physically smaller than Jack, but fish grew to adulthood sooner than men, and they had an independence he could only dream of. Their mother might have had something to do with that, too, Jack thought. She wasn't at all like Aunt Ermie.

The gig glided into Plymouth harbor, skirting around bits of floating detritus. Jack tried to imagine Georgie swimming there, near the place where fishermen loaded empty nets into their boats. The sight turned Jack's stomach, but he hid his queasiness well, not that anyone was looking at him. The rowers shipped oars and the boat nosed onto the beach. Jack leaped out the moment they touched land, tossed the pilot a coin, and was on his way.

§

Jack hurried past the fish market, where a boy hawker advertised his wares.

"Medicine, medicine," the boy called. "Geronimo's cure for what ails! Stills the stomach, eases the mind! Geronimo's cure! Medicine!"

Even in the long years when Aunt Ermie had had him convinced that his mother was a dead Plymouth whore, Jack had never been able to stomach fish, or even sit in the room when it was being eaten. His fingers curled around the conch shell his mother had given him. In a blind alley just outside the market, he touched it to his ear.

The whoosh of sea waves greeted him. Jack listened for a moment, whoosh and fade, whoosh and fade. There it was, he thought, an ordinary conch shell. Maybe he had been dreaming, after all. Then a tinny voice pinged in over the noise: "Help, help! Oh, my gills, my poor gills."

Jack straightened and turned towards the sound. Where was it coming from? He stepped out of the shadows and into the market.

Fishmonger's boxes overflowed with last night's catch. Women, housekeepers like Aunt Ermie, glanced sidelong at the wares as they passed, baskets clean, noses sharp. Jack wove through the market, shell to his ear, hearing the agony of the fishes more clearly than ever before. There were minnows and carp, cod and plaice, mackerel and porgies. There they were! The porgies, their mellifluous voices bubbling clear into the landsmen's air, crying in agony. Jack ventured closer and stood still to listen.

"Hey, you there!" the fishmonger shouted.

Jack pulled the conch from his ear and looked at the red-faced man who was shouting and making shooing motions at him.

"I'm sorry," Jack said. "What did you say?"

"Are you listening? I said move on! You're driving away my best customers."

Cruel-hearted, that's what he was, Jack thought. Couldn't he see the agony of the fishes?

"I didn't hear you before." Jack cringed. Even here in the market, people noticed his smell. The purse-lipped women held back, eying him distastefully, clearly wondering if it were the fish or the man who stank so pungently.

"Well, you hear me now. Be on your way!"

Jack shook his head. "I'm looking for a porgie. You have more here than the other fishmongers."

"'Course I do, caught all with my own nets, by my own good sons, right here in Plymouth, not lying about in a boat's bottom like some men have them, what's it to you? Pick one and be gone."

Jack leaned in closer and set the conch to his ear again. He looked at the fish, layered on top of one another, gills fluttering, eyes going flat.

Georgie had been a bit like them, he remembered now, a solid oblong of a fish, with shimmering silver scales and hints of iridescence. His fins had been fine and sharp like these, though he had a more pointed snout than most porgies. He had been a fine fish, just as Jack looked like a fine young man, but the other fish had kept their distance from him. He, too, had been different. Of the three of them, Thomas had been most comfortable with the creatures who looked like him.

"Hurry up, now!" the fishmonger shouted into Jack's ear. "What size fish do you want?"

"I think he was on the bigger side," Jack said.

"He?" the fishmonger said. "Go, get out of here!"

"Just one moment!" Jack pleaded. The fish looked up at him. He bent down to them and whispered, bubbles coming out of his mouth.

"*The fish who smells like a man, do you know him?*" Jack whispered into the shell.

The fish flapped madly. *"Help us! Release us!"*

"I want to, I do, but where is he, my brother?"

"That stinky one, we saw him, gone with the woman with the long, red fingers, gone yesterday. They gutted him, just here, and the dogs came and ate the rest. Release us!"

"Gone!" Jack looked up. The fishmonger had a knife in his hand, and was standing very close indeed.

"Now which do you want?" he said. "I'll clean it for you."

"No, no, that won't be necessary!" Jack reached into the bin and took three fish, the first his fingers closed around, wishing he could take them all. "I'll take these!" he said. "With some of your seaweed…"

Jack made a pocket out of his oilskins and tucked the fish inside. He gave the fishmonger a fistful of coins before he fled, hoping that it was the right amount. It was like paying a murderer. He ran for the harbor and straight to the end of the pier. The tide flowed swiftly out. They could ride it back to sea.

"Go! Swim far from here!" he said. He tossed the fish, one by one, into the tide.

He watched them go, diving back to their accustomed depths, struggling, but struggling strongly enough that he dared to hope for their survival. He closed his eyes and prayed that they would skirt the fishermen's nets. He walked back to the shore, then on along the quayside towards town. He wondered if the fish had heard him, if they'd understood anything he'd said at all. A red-fingered woman. Damn her, Jack thought, there was no telling who she had been, and no help for Georgie any more, in any case.

Thomas might be in London, his mother had said, if she were to be trusted, if she weren't only a dream. It was time to go to London. He couldn't do anything more for those fish. He had to find Thomas. Father had given him money, meant for courting a young woman and buying himself a new suit of clothes, as if that would be enough to find him a bride. It was enough to cover Jack's ticket to London and back, at least, if he kept his purse-strings tight while he was there.

§

On Sydney Street, Aunt Ermentrude would be putting coffee on. She would have porridge and hot sausages. His stomach grumbled, but he couldn't bear facing Aunt Ermie today. She would not be pleased about his mermaid mother, if he could even tell her about it. Oh, botheration. *Jack* wasn't pleased. Perhaps he should look in on his aunt before setting out for London, or perhaps not.

Just before the end of the harbor, he decided to test his shell again, to hear what the sea would say. He took off his socks and shoes, rolled his trousers up and waded in right there in front of the whole town. It felt strangely comfortable, standing up to his knees in water. Experimentally, he bent his naked ear to the water and listened. A wavelet slapped his neck. He batted it away. He put the shell to his ear and tried again to listen to the sea.

"Jack!" he thought he heard a woman's voice, scolding.

He put his mouth to the conch and whispered, "Mother?" Then he listened again. All he could hear were the waves.

"Jack!" the voice came again. This time he looked up towards the quayside.

"Oh. Hello, Mrs. Beaton."

"What on earth are you doing there?" she said. "Have you lost something?" Mrs. Beaton was one of those women who liked to keep a finger in her neighbors' business, despite having seven half-grown children of her own.

"Nothing important…" Jack said. He looked into the water as if searching for something, and hoped she hadn't noticed the conch.

"That's a very pretty shell you have there," she commented as he waded towards her.

"Thank you," he said. "I was just visiting my father."

"I suppose we'll be seeing you on Sydney Street shortly?"

"Oh." Jack tried to think, but he was too disoriented by being half in the water and talking to the very land-minded Mrs. Beaton, who would report back to his equally land-locked aunt. "No," he decided. "No, I don't think I will see you. You see I've got urgent business. In… in London. Would you mind? Could you tell Aunt Ermie that I'll be a few days yet?" he said. "I'm so glad I ran into you," he added, to try to be polite. He wished that she would just move on and leave him to his listening.

"Glad to have seen you, too," said Mrs. Beaton, with a frown. "I'd change out of those wet trousers if I were you. Even in summer, a man can catch a chill like that."

"Thank you. Of course, Mrs. Beaton," Jack said. He plunged his hands into his pockets and looked down into the water, hoping that Mrs. Beaton would go away before he changed his mind and went to Aunt Ermie's, after all, to a respectable breakfast and the afternoon train to Bristol and his accountancy course.

Mrs. Beaton walked ever so slowly up the quay, glancing back from time to time. Other people stared at him, too, but he watched the minnows until she was out of sight. Then he waded to shore and made straight for the train station. He most certainly would not change his trousers. By the time he reached the station, his cuffs were only slightly damp anyway. A train's whistle blew. It was the nine o'clock to London.

§

Jack slipped past the closing gate and jumped onto the step of the last coach. The conductor took his ticket at arm's length and wrinkled his nose. No one wanted to stand near him, but there was nothing new about that. He tucked the ticket into his pocket and swayed down the length of the train, looking for a seat. Every compartment seemed to be full. He'd only been to London once, a few years ago, with Aunt Ermie. They had stayed in a modest house on the outskirts of the metropolis, and he'd seen very little of the city. It was a much bigger place than Plymouth, though. He would doubtless be lost before he'd walked half a mile, let alone before he found his brother.

He passed a compartment full of young men

bent over a game of cards. There was no room, even if he would have been welcome there. Jack didn't even know how to play cards. The people in the accountancy course certainly wouldn't approve of such company, anyway.

The train's motion made Jack queasy. It wasn't like the sea. Just before his empty-stomached queasiness overwhelmed him, he found a compartment that wasn't full. There were only two passengers inside: an elderly gentleman with a barrister's brief case, and a young woman with a shawl over her shoulders. She gazed out the window, as if not hearing – or smelling – his arrival. The gentleman wrinkled his nose and looked sharply at Jack.

"Excuse me," Jack said, "is that seat taken?"

"Yes," he said. "My associates are joining me at the next station. Would you be so kind as to move on?"

Jack was about to do just that when the young woman turned to look at him. She cocked her head to one side and looked at him intently for a breathless moment before speaking. "There is plenty of room here at the moment," she said. "I am sure you can sit here until the other passengers arrive."

It was so unexpected, for a lady to invite him to sit. Jack froze.

"Why in that case, I... I... I will sit, thank you ever so much." He turned to the gentleman. "I will move on directly when your associates arrive," Jack promised.

The gentleman harrumphed and unfurled his newspaper, blocking the two other passengers from his sight. Jack settled himself into the seat opposite the young lady, beside the window. He watched the tracks disappear behind them, the familiar environs of Plymouth slipping away. The young lady continued to gaze out the window, but Jack felt as if she were watching him. It was not an unpleasant sensation. Jack hoped he would find Thomas alive somewhere, ideally near the train station in London, but how would he know Thomas? The tracks clicked past.

Jack worked up the courage to look at his fellow passenger again. The side-view of her face was quite pretty, and she had spared him a kind word but if she had looked his way at all it was out of the corner of her eye, and quietly. He could think of nothing to say to her in any case. She continued to clutch her shawl around her shoulders despite the growing heat of the day. He pulled his thoughts away from her. He ought to be concentrating on coming up with a plan, some sort of a system for finding Thomas, but his thoughts were muddled, leading nowhere.

The train rolled into the next station and the next and still the old gentleman sat alone behind his newspaper. A few people wandered by, opened the door, sniffed, and moved on. As the train rolled away from the third station, the young lady looked up.

"I don't believe you do have any associates coming along," she said, directly to the man's screen of newsprint.

"I beg your pardon!" the gentleman snapped his newspaper shut. He had a clip on his nose.

Jack stifled a laugh.

"Intolerable!" the gentleman huffed. "I intend to complain to the conductor." He gathered up his case and wig and departed, slamming the compartment door behind him.

The young lady turned to stare out the window again, but after a moment she glanced at Jack enquiringly.

"Sir?" she said.

"Yes, ma'am, at your service," Jack spouted.

"Do you wonder, just now, why that man had a clip on his nose?"

Jack blushed and noticed that his shoes were due for a polish. "No, I don't. I imagine it was on account of the smell."

"What smell?" the young lady asked. "I'm afraid my nose isn't very sharp."

"Really?" Jack brightened. He smiled, and his back straightened. "I... I don't know what to say."

"So, what is it?" the lady queried.

"I... it's... it's nothing," Jack said. "It's just that I have a... some people say I have an unpleasant odor, rather like a fish."

"That is unkind of them," the young lady said. "I don't mind fish. In fact, I rather like them, so pretty, when they swim," she said wistfully. Jack wondered if she liked to eat them, too, but he put the thought out of his mind as she leaned forward. "May I know your name?" she asked.

Jack introduced himself. The young lady's name was Miss Parker, and she was also going to London, where she said that she lived part of the time.

"Otherwise, I travel about some," she said vaguely. She volunteered no other information about herself. They had tea and sandwiches from a cart. He asked her about London, and she asked him where he lived. He told her about his studies in Bristol, and though accountancy didn't turn most girl's hearts aflutter, she listened attentively. It was the most delightful day of his entire land-bound existence.

§

Jack's mood darkened as they entered the outskirts of London in that afternoon. He'd been flirting the day away without a thought of Thomas.

The train rolled into Waterloo Station. The hubbub outside hit Jack like a gale wind. He clutched his hat as the train slowed.

"What brings you to London?" Miss Parker shouted over the screech of the brakes. She leaned over to pull a weathered portmanteau out from under her seat.

"Oh, a sort of a family matter," Jack stammered. "A quest, if you will."

"A quest!" Miss Parker clapped her hands, leaving the case on the floor. "I love quests." Then she frowned. "I'm not so sure about family matters."

"I don't know much about them, myself," Jack said. "I'm practically an orphan... well, not exactly, but my maiden aunt raised me. I'm looking for a... another member of the family, after a fashion."

New passengers were converging on the carriage doors. "We'd better hurry if we're going to get off," Miss Parker said. She stood with one long fluid motion. She was taller than Jack had expected, almost as tall as himself, and her grey dress rippled down past her ankles in waves, then smoothed into a satin stillness just above the floor. She leaned over and gave the portmanteau a mighty tug, then tried to push it out of their compartment on the floor. As she struggled with it, her shawl slipped, revealing a large grey patch of skin at the base of her neck. She pulled the shawl up and glanced anxiously at Jack.

"Let me help with that," Jack offered. "I'll carry it for you, wherever you like to go." He hadn't meant to say that. He had meant to bid her good afternoon, and get back to his search for Thomas. Miss Parker could probably help him find his way, he told himself. She would be as knowledgeable a guide as he could hope for.

She blushed. "I'm sure I can manage."

"Or I can hail a porter?" Jack offered.

"No, that's quite alright," she shook her head adamantly. "No need for a porter. You can help me part of the way, I suppose."

Jack lifted the case up onto his shoulder. It was almost too heavy for him to carry, but he could manage it. Something clinked and sloshed faintly inside, glass wrapped in wool, he guessed, but beyond that what was it? He wondered if his conch would help him hear that, too. He followed Miss Parker down the corridor of the train carriage. She stood anxiously on the platform as he climbed down from the train. As soon as he had his footing on the platform, Jack checked his pocket for the conch, which was still there, safe and secure. He relaxed his grip ever so slightly... and the case slid off his shoulder. He almost panicked, but caught the portmanteau an inch before it hit the ground.

"Watch yourself there, man!" a passerby grumbled.

Miss Parker clapped both of her hands over her mouth. Her eyebrows froze in an arch halfway up to her hairline.

"Oh dear," she breathed. "Do you think anything broke?"

Jack listened as he crouched there among the scurrying knees and boots, the train squealing back into motion behind him. "No," he said. "I think it's all right. What is it?"

"It's nothing really. I can get it," she said.

"No," Jack countered. "No, I insist. I'll be more careful."

Miss Parker set her hands on the case and looked at Jack. "Are you sure?"

Jack looked into her eyes. They were green. "Yes. Quite sure."

"Well, let's go, then," she said. She cut a confident swath through the crowd. Jack scurried to keep up, following her through the station to a little alley which spilled out onto a path beside the river. Jack exhaled, then took a deep breath of the smell of water flowing past. Not salt water, but it would do after their long, dry railway journey.

"Miss, Miss!" Jack said. "Would you mind? I mean, your case is quite heavy. Could we..."

She turned around, looking slightly sheepish. "Oh, I'm sorry. Yes, of course we could rest." She walked back to Jack and helped him ease the portmanteau to the ground. She listened to it carefully as it clinked to the paving stones. "You're right, I don't think there is anything broken."

Jack nodded, then paused to look at the river

and smell it more deeply. It was awash with people on bridges, on boats, on barges and on ships, sluicing to and fro between the banks and up and down the river, not to mention all the smells of the populace crowded too close along its banks. He wondered how a porpoise could swim through that melee and not get run over, or choke on some bit of refuse. He felt the shell in his pocket, but wasn't sure he that wanted Miss Parker to see it. She would think it odd. Who wouldn't?

"You said you have a quest?" Miss Parker prompted, sitting down on her portmanteau.

"Oh, actually I'm looking for a porpoise."

"A purpose? But you have a quest!"

"A porpoise," Jack said. "You know, grey, swim in the river."

"A porpoise?" Miss Parker said at last. "Why did you come to London for that? I'm quite certain I saw porpoises in the river at Plymouth."

"Well, it's a particular porpoise," Jack said, blushing. "Look, never mind about that. What's in this case of yours? It's awfully heavy."

She looked away. "It's not very interesting."

"Books?" Jack ventured.

"Yes. A few books. And other things. I took them down to Plymouth for my father but we didn't have many buyers there, the boy said."

"The boy? What boy?"

She sighed. "It hardly matters. I can take it from here," she said. "I'll just get a hackney to our wagon."

"Wagon?" Jack said.

"Oh, I've said too much," Miss Parker wailed. "Here you were, thinking I was a respectable young lady."

"But you are," Jack said, "aren't you?" If she were a trollop, surely he would have some sense of misgiving by now, or she would have plied him with strong drink, or other tools of seduction. Miss Parker was really quite different from any other female he'd come across, not stern like his aunt and her neighbors, nor scornful like the young ladies at his college.

Miss Parker hung her head. "No, not really. I'm just a peddler."

"You're very well spoken, for a peddler," Jack said.

"Father sent me to Miss Jones's Academy, when mother... Well, I do have a proper education. And, well..." Miss Parker gripped the handle and hefted the portmanteau unsteadily. "Thank you for your help, but I think I'll carry it now."

Jack took the handle from the other side. Her grip was strong, but she wasn't pulling away from him, not really.

"I'm sure the books will be fine," he said.

She shook her head and let Jack take the case. "It's the bottles, though. They'd break and soak everything and we only have these hundred left."

"Bottles? Bottles of what?" Jack asked.

"Geronimo's Magical Elixir..." she said, looking at her feet.

"Cures what ails you?" Jack said. "I saw the boy with the billboard beside the fish market... in Plymouth." Plymouth seemed like it was a lifetime away, instead of only a half day's journey behind him.

Miss Parker nodded. "It can cure everything,

really it can, I mean, it cured my stutter, even, though sometimes I forget and don't like to talk to strangers anyway, and that's why I'm not a very good peddler, though that boy isn't very good, either. I really should get back to Father's wagon."

"Is it a wild west wagon?" Jack asked. "I've always wanted to see one. Ships of the prairie, they call them, though I don't really know what a prairie looks like, either. It must be at least a little like the sea, if they call the wagons ships."

"You could, but Father... Well, I can't account for what Father might say, or do."

"I can never account for my father, either," Jack said, "despite the course."

She looked at him blankly.

"In accountancy. At the college in Bristol. Accounting, account for... never mind."

She laughed, slowly at first, then building into teary-eyed mirth.

"No it's really very funny," she said at last. "But honestly, your father can't be as bad as mine."

"Oh, he can," Jack said.

She smiled tentatively. "You don't mind? I mean, we have a bit of a medicine show. It's not a respectable trade at all, if you ask most people."

"No, I'm sure it's fine with me, I..." He gazed up into her eyes. They were still moist from her teary laughter, softening the green color which complemented her auburn hair and fair skin, though maybe her nose was a little larger than fashionable. "I quite like..."

"Medicine shows? Everyone does. Let's go, then." She strode off along the river bank. Jack shouldered the case as quickly as he could and lengthened his stride to catch up. Occasionally, he cast a glance toward the river, hoping to see porpoises, but mostly he had to keep looking ahead and dodging through the throngs which threatened to swallow Miss Parker up and leave him lost, with nothing but a case of elixir and maybe a broken heart.

"I say, your father isn't Geronimo himself, is he?" Jack asked once, when he had almost caught up with her.

Miss Parker shook her head. "Not exactly," she said. "He made the elixir, but couldn't sell any at first. He said, 'Charlie Parker's Potion just doesn't have the right ring to it. We'll have to re-formulate the label.'"

She quickened her pace, occasionally looking over her shoulder to make sure Jack was still behind her. What if she *were* a trollop, or worse? One of his classmates in Bristol said that her cousin's pockets had been fleeced clean by pickpockets within an hour of arriving in London, and another said that a friend of his had woken up behind a tavern with only his underclothes on. Jack had told her that he would carry the portmanteau, though, and so he would. Besides, he wanted to know where she would lead him, almost as badly as he wanted to find Thomas. He was also not quite ready to dive into the Thames, with its high banks and deafening traffic. Then he would have only the shell in his pocket between himself and near-certain death.`

§

CHAPTER THREE: CARNIVAL MEN

They walked for miles and miles. Jack had no idea how to get back to the station. It wasn't evening yet, but the gloom of the smoke overhead darkened a little with the afternoon, and Jack wondered where he would stay the night. He supposed there must be boarding houses or inns someplace. After some time, Miss Parker turned away from the river and entered an area of ramshackle tenements with open places like missing teeth between them, and a few worn nubs of old houses here and there. It was not a respectable sort of neighborhood. She rounded a corner into a dark alley. A moment later they emerged into a vacant, refuse-strewn lot, which might be thought to loosely resemble a prairie. Very loosely.

"There it is," she announced. Jack set down the case and stopped to take it all in. The wagon looked like a cross between a gypsy caravan and a settler's wagon, but with more of the former and less of the later, no matter what Charlie Parker's intentions had been. Across the top someone had painted "Geronimo's Magical Elixir" in bright red letters, but on the side-rails Jack could see the words "Charlie Parker's Potion" through a thin layer of paint. A curl of smoke rose from the wagon's stovepipe and a mangy horse greeted Miss Parker with a snort.

"Father has the supper on," Miss Parker said. "That's a good sign."

Jack looked at her sidelong. She was sniffing the air quite deliberately. On a turn of the breeze, Jack could just catch the smell of potatoes boiling... and a whiff of rotting fish besides.

"Maybe I'd better go look for lodgings," Jack said.

"Nonsense. If the fire's on, that's supper, and you've come all this way, so you'd might as well meet father. He wouldn't like to hear that you'd helped me and ducked out. I mean..." She blushed again.

Jack worried. It did sound a bit like one of those stories where hospitality masks a robber's plans, but he liked Miss Parker, and he had the impression that she liked him, too.

"I really ought to be on with my quest," he said. The fishy smell grew stronger.

"Who's there?" bellowed a voice from inside the caravan.

"It's only me, Father," Miss Parker said, advancing towards the caravan. Jack followed her closely. "I've brought a guest, so make yourself decent."

"If only I can get this beast to eat something!"

the voice inside grumbled. "Aren't porpoises supposed to eat fish?"

Jack's uneasiness quickened to a panic. His heart raced. His hands shook.

"I'd better be going," he said, but what he really wanted to do was to push Miss Parker out of the way and rush into the wagon to find out what on earth was happening there.

"Nonsense," Miss Parker said, oblivious, "you've come all this way." She opened the door. "Father, meet..." She gave Jack a blank, panicked stare. "... a gentleman I met on the train..." she said faintly. "Oh, dear."

Jack had gone quite white in the face, blanched. A dying porpoise lay on the wagon floor. You didn't have to be half-fish to see that see it was dying. Jack bent over it and tried to hear its heartbeat, while Charlie Parker held forth, oblivious to his guest's – and his daughter's – discomfort.

"There was a fellow down by Gravesend last week, Doctor Washington's Wonders, has a lousy show, he doesn't even know half the tricks in my book," he babbled. "I've got 'em all, all the tricks of the trade, but suddenly folks from as far away as Oxford were talking about Doctor Washington, said he'd got himself a pair of talking fish. Well, they were coming from far and wide and I could hardly let that go. I put on my old lady disguise and went down there. You'd never believe it. There he had this porpoise spouting the Queen's English, well, one of 'em anyhow. He said the other one had laryngitis. I never saw such a thing. Had to get me one..."

The medicine show man would have gone on talking, but a parrot interrupted him with: "Queen's English, Queen's English!"

"Dr. Washington, you say?" Jack said. He touched the porpoise. Her pulse fluttered under his hand.

"That's the name."

Jack held the dying porpoise in his arms and bit back his anger. The porpoise was heavy. If there was a talking porpoise at Gravesend, it had to be Thomas, he thought. The rumor, this sudden hope, drove all thoughts of romanceout of his mind, not to mention fear of kidnapping.

"What happened?" Jack said, keeping his hand steady on the porpoise.

"Well, I'm glad you asked," Charlie Parker rattled on in his best showman's voice. "I thought, I have to get me one of them fish, so I sent Iris here out of town and hurried over to Gravesend yesterday afternoon."

"Is that what it was?" Miss Parker snapped. "I should have known you were up to no good!"

"Don't interrupt, Iris. The show must go on!"

The porpoise in Jack's arms flapped dully. Jack stroked her head. Iris was a beautiful name. It suited Miss Parker perfectly.

"As I was saying, I went on down to the lousy blighter's caravan and had me in mind to... let's just say I thought I might borrow his fish for a little while, take the wind out of his sails, so to speak, the horse from his wagon, that kind of thing. But when I got there it was all quiet-like, stone cold, that show of his. They had a tank where the porpoises had been living and there was one of 'em belly up. Belly up. I didn't even see the other one."

Jack sank his head into his hands. He heard the medicine show man's voice as if from a great distance.

"So I said, I'll get me another one, train it up. Just last night I got this one out of the river, hauled it up, I did. Here you see, but not a word out of him yet."

Jack pulled himself up, grabbed the man by his sequined lapel and shook him. "This porpoise is dying!" he shouted into Charlie Parker's bewildered face. "You probably killed her. Let her go, back to the river."

"Her? And how do you know this is a lady porpoise, young man?" Iris's father asked, recovering his bluster. "Maybe that's the trouble with this one. Women. So temperamental," he chuckled.

Jack leaned in close to the porpoise. "Save me," she said. Iris held her father back. Jack understood the porpoise's words without even reaching for his conch shell.

"I'll take you to the river," he whispered to her. It came out all fishy. The porpoise understood. So did Iris's father, but in a different way.

"Now, now, young man," he said gently. "You can't just walk in here and start taking my show pieces, my hard-won show pieces away." Jack shook his head and tried to lift the porpoise toward the door, but she was as heavy as himself. "I see you're a special young man, uniquely talented, even," said Charlie Parker, alias Geronimo. "I can help you. You've got a great career ahead of you if you stick with me."

Jack wouldn't have listened at all, but Iris tugged his sleeve. "And me," she said.

"And, what?" Jack asked her.

"Stick with me, and father..." Iris said.

"I can't!" Jack said. "I need to borrow your horse!"

"No sir, you will not!" Charlie Parker shouted. He shook his fist at Jack.

Jack heaved backwards and stumbled down the steps, pulling the porpoise by her fins. The porpoise flapped down on top of him, pushing all the wind from his lungs, then rolled onto the ground beside him, breathing but weak.

"She's dying!" Jack repeated.

He felt Iris's hand on his shoulder. "I'll help you get the porpoise to the river," she said. "It's not far."

Jack nodded. "I'd be most obliged." He couldn't quite bear to look at her, though. He had been fooled. Iris may not have been trying to lay a trap for him, but her father would, given half a chance.

The porpoise looked up at Jack, desperation in her eyes.

Jack tried to mumble comfort to the dying creature. He looked up to find both Miss Parker and her father regarding him hungrily.

"Go away!" Jack said.

"Well that's a fine thing for a man to say on another man's doorstep, but I won't say the same to you," Charlie Parker said. He turned to his daughter. "You've done well, for once. A young man! Imagine that. Just the young man for you."

"I rather think that's for me to decide. Or not," Miss Parker said stonily. She unhitched the mangy horse and led it to Jack and the porpoise.

"Come on, then," she said. "Let's go."

They hefted the porpoise over the nag's back, working together in a harmony which startled Jack. It was a strange and blissful moment, a unity of mind which made him realize how strained and awkward every single social interaction in his life had been before he'd met Iris that morning. He still couldn't look her in the eye, though, not with her father glaring at them like that.

The porpoise relaxed into a curve across the horse's back, overcome with exhaustion.

"Miss Parker," Jack stammered, "Miss Parker, I'm most obliged."

"It's no more than you did for me," she said. Jack felt something tightening in him. Hastily, he re-focused his attention on the porpoise. Iris, marvel of a young lady that she was, slapped the horse's rump.

"Don't you go off with that man!" her father yelled as they crossed the vacant lot.

Iris hesitated. She ran back to the caravan, pushed her father aside, and emerged a moment later carrying a sword.

"That's my best sword. Here, now!" Charlie Parker shook his fist, but made no move to stop her. She tucked the sword into her sash and ran back to Jack and the horse. The porpoise flapped faintly.

"I really... your family obligation?" Jack stammered.

"Oh, don't mind Father. He's got no use for this. Besides, it's mine. It belonged to my mother's father." Iris took the horse's bridle and urged it into the street.

The afternoon sun slipped behind the tenements and a deeper gloom started to settle over the neighborhood. Jack kept one hand on the porpoise, whispering to her with sounds of comfort he now remembered from his infancy. Iris prodded the horse forward. A short turn along another alley led them to a muddy embankment. The horse plodded on, halfway down to the swirling waters, then skidded and fell to her knees. Jack lunged forward to steady the porpoise.

"I can smell it," the porpoise said. "I'm nearly, nearly..."

"Oh, botheration!" Iris said to the horse.

Jack looked up, startled. Botheration? Now that was strong language for a gently bred young lady, though not strong enough for a true carnival huckster.

The porpoise flapped. Jack bent to get his arms under her body, to ease her into a soft part of the mud. He looked up at Iris. "Can you... Can you lift her tail, do you think?"

Iris nodded. The horse stood still except for twitching her ears. A gaggle of beggars and snotty-nosed infants peered at them from the shelter of the nearby tenements.

Iris glanced up at them and grumbled. "Good thing Father isn't here."

"Well, yes, but why?" Jack asked.

"He'd have me pass the hat to those people. As if they have a penny among them!"

"Indeed," Jack said. He had to admit that Iris's father was possibly even less respectable than his own. Being the keeper of the Eddystone Light might make a man half mad, but at least it was a steady government job.

The porpoise's pulse quickened as they splashed into the shallow water. Jack looked into her eyes. She was delirious and near death, or at least gravely ill. But he had to ask.

"Bbblbble" he seemed to say.

"No, I don't know your brother," the porpoise replied, "but splash! Home. Splash!"

Jack and Iris watched the porpoise inch out into the Thames. A weak cheer went up behind them.

"There, now!" Charlie Parker's voice bellowed. "There now there! She was the last of the show, the last of a great race..."

Iris whipped around. "Be quiet, Father! For God's sake!"

Jack looked on in disgust as Charlie Parker took off his had and tried to press the watching children for coins.

Iris shook her head. "He can't help himself."

"I see," Jack muttered. "I don't know what to do."

"Well, go!" Iris said. "Don't you have a quest?"

"Well, yes... it's just that... I don't know... Could you tell me the way to Gravesend? And how I will find this Doctor Washington and his so-called Wonders?"

She took the sword from her belt and pointed it.

"That way. Along the river. Now go!"

Jack nodded. "Thank you. Thank you. I hope we meet again."

Iris caught her breath. "You'd better take this, too," she said. She handed him the sword.

Jack had never felt more like a fish out of water

than he did as she pressed the sword hilt into his hand. "I don't think I know what to do with this."

The river gurgled, laughing at him.

"Iris, get back here!" her father yelled.

"Coming, Father!"

And then she was gone.

Jack stood alone, watching the river roll by, sword in hand.

He set out for Gravesend and, perhaps, his brother's dead body.

§

By the time Jack found the ferry to Gravesend – which was nearly as far from the caravan as the train station had been – night and a soupy fog had fallen. He picked his way down the cobbled street towards the river and stepped onto the quayside.

"Greenwich, Gravesend, all aboard!" he heard. The ferry puffed and chugged. He sprinted after it, but there was a barrier, then another, and he had to go around, and by the time he reached the dock, the boat was a hundred yards downriver. He looked after it and let his bag slump to the dock.

"There'll be another at midnight," said a boy, startling him from behind. When Jack turned to look at him, the boy held out a hand. Did he expect a penny for the information? Jack could just as easily have read it from the noticeboard, but then, he hadn't. He dug in his pocket, then caught a glimpse of another urchin making a grab for his bag.

His hand fell on the hilt of his sword.

"Now there," Jack said. "I'm armed, so off with

you!" His voice rang out like that of a man people might take heed of, rather than in his usual, cautious tones.

The boy's eyes widened. "Pardon me, sir!"

The bag-snatcher slipped back into the shadows.

Jack looked down at his hand, which had moved to the hilt of the rapier almost of its own accord. He wouldn't have thought to draw the blade, would he? He wondered why Iris had given it to him. She had taken it into her head to help him, or that she owed him something, but surely the service of carrying a case three miles through London didn't merit a sword as a reward.

Jack yawned. He hadn't slept much the night before and had only napped for a moment on the train. He settled himself on a bench in the waiting room and dozed until the next ferry came, keeping the sword across his lap.

He sleepily handed over money for the ticket and climbed aboard a few hours later, found another seat and fell back into a fitful doze, half-aware of the chugging engine and waking every now and again to brush soot off his face. He listened to the gurgle of water underneath. Memories churned to the surface of his mind and tumbled back under: Thomas and Georgie swimming up to the rocks, his mother gathering them together, and teaching him to swim. They were all infant memories, things he ought not have remembered at all, things he thought he had forgotten. He half-dreamed of his mother the night before, combing phosphorescence through her hair and of Iris, knighting him with the sword instead of just handing it to him. He had just fallen into a deep sleep when the ferry jarred into a dock and a rough hand shook him.

"Was it Gravesend you wanted?" the ferryman grunted.

"Yes, sir, yes," Jack replied. "Thank you for waking me."

"It's end of the line. You can sleep here another hour, but you'll have to pay."

Jack shook his head and hastily gathered his things. "No, no thank you. I'll be off."

The ferryman frowned. "Nowhere to go, this time of the night."

"It's nearly dawn," Jack observed.

The ferryman shrugged. "Have it your way, then."

"Would you kindly direct me to the market, or the fairgrounds? If there is one?"

"There'll be no one about, this time of night. Give us a tuppence and stay aboard." The ferryman held out a greasy hand, and smiled with a twitch of his lip. Jack was fully awake now, and it seemed that whatever menace Gravesend held could hardly exceed the ferryman's thinly veiled invitation to be robbed. Jack took a firm grip of his bag, set the other hand on the hilt of his sword, and leaped out onto the docks.

Ships' masts listed ghostly in the moonlight. Rats scuttled through the shadows. Gaslights burned at the corners, with their unlit fellows menacing the streets in between. Jack found the terminus of the tram line and set about looking for a timetable. Of course there was nothing posted, and only a small bit of roof to shelter under. He sat on the bench there. His trousers were creased and he itched with the grime of London. He scratched his outer thigh, which felt rough underneath the cloth. He would not let himself fall asleep and be confused with a drunk, collapsed and waiting to have any lingering pennies picked from his pockets.

At length, there was a clatter from one of the nearby trams, followed by the lighting of a match, and a raised lantern. Inside the tram, the driver set his cap on and dusted off his jacket.

Jack met him at the steps of the tram.

"Pardon me, sir, but could you direct me to the fairgrounds."

"The fairgrounds?" The driver looked at him with a raised eyebrow.

"I'm looking for a Dr. Washington."

The driver frowned and stroked his trim beard. "I think you're better to look elsewhere."

"Oh, no. I'm looking for someone, you see. Someone in particular. I heard that Dr. Washington might know his whereabouts?"

The driver shrugged. "So long as you know what you're about." Then he sniffed and frowned. "You're of that ilk, then."

"I'm sorry, I don't know what..."

"You know I have to sleep in this tram half the nights of the week, but I do make an effort at hygiene."

Of all the insults as he'd suffered for his smell, few had been so direct, and most had been whispered behind his back. All the confidence Iris had puffed into him leaked out in a dismal sigh. Confidence or no, he had to find Thomas.

"The direction to the fairgrounds, if you please,"

Jack said, summoning every inch of posture he could muster.

The tram driver pointed, holding a handkerchief over his nose. Jack returned to the shelter to pick up his bag and sword. Behind him, he heard a clatter as the tram driver dropped his keys to the pavement.

"A sword. He's a madman, by god," the driver said.

Jack belted it on and walked away.

§

At the fairgrounds' gate, his heart was racing and the itch of his skin, particularly on his outer thighs, had become quite uncomfortable. He clutched the handle of the rapier. The gate was locked, of course. He abandoned respectability and clambered over the fence a few yards down where there was a convenient overhanging tree, its bark worn smooth from all the other entry attempts it had assisted.

As he landed on the inside of the fence, a distant ship's horn sounded. It was a mile away if it was a yard. Jack felt that he was far, much too far, from the river. Fog wreathed through the carnival attractions veiling the garish colors of false fronts looming overhead. Deep within the fairgrounds, a lone donkey brayed its complaints.

Jack followed the sound of the donkey trumpeting and thumping against the sides of its pen. He crept along in the shadows, as if one of the painted faces might wake and wag its eyebrows at him. The donkey found a tin pail to kick, the sound of which finally roused its keeper.

"Shut yer gob or I'll muzzle ya," a gravelly voice declared, from just the other side of the thin wall Jack had been walking along. Jack jumped sideways, straight into a shallow but messy puddle. Mud splashed up his rumpled trousers. One dab of mud landed below the cuff, on his ankle, and for a moment, that one spot didn't itch. He longed for a bit of water to ease the rest of his legs in.

He stepped away from the wall and read the marquee beside him: "Doctor Washington's Wonders." He took a deep breath, raised his hand, and thumped the side of the caravan at the spot where the voice had just complained.

"What's it now, Bertie?" the voice said.

Jack cleared his throat. "Doctor Washington, I presume?" he asked feebly.

Two eyes in the painting beside him flicked open.

"Who're you?"

Jack straightened his shoulders. "I've come looking for a porpoise, sir. I understand you had talking porpoises here lately."

"What's it to you? You one of those animal lovers?"

Jack's hand went to the rapier's hilt. "I'd appreciate it if you'd show me to your porpoises, sir."

Jack heard a clatter in one of the neighboring caravans and another pair of painted eyes popped open across the packed-dirt path.

"Go 'way, Bertie," Doctor Washington – if that was indeed the man's name – said.

"Have it your way.," the voice snarled. Jack's grip tightened on his sword.

A hidden door opened at the end of the caravan. Doctor Washington stood there in a nightshirt, regarding Jack balefully.

"I s'pose it was you roused Emma?"

"Emma?"

"The donkey. Says so right on her collar."

"I wouldn't know, haven't seen her," Jack explained. "I came the other way 'round."

"Did you?" Doctor Washington said, as if calling Jack a bald-faced liar. He was bald-headed and of medium height. He had tobacco stains on his fingers and looked to be about as undistinguished a man as Jack had ever seen.

From inside the caravan, Jack could hear the rustle of wings, a scratching at cages, and the desolate complaints of many animals housed in too-close quarters. There was also water nearby. He could smell its stagnation, the scent of death in it.

"The porpoise..."

Doctor Washington waved his hand. "I told you, I have no truck with your lot."

Jack drew his sword.

"But armaments, now that puts a new wrinkle on the matter."

"Does it?" Jack said. "So then, where is he? Where are they, I mean."

Doctor Washington jerked his thumb towards the far end of his marquee. Jack narrowed his eyes at Doctor Washington, then dashed to the end of the caravan.

A large, squat tub, like a truncated barrel, stood full of green water, surrounded by a flat stage on shaky struts. A rope ladder was tied to it with a devilish-looking knot. Jack took his sword and cut through cord, letting it roll down so that he could climb up... for all the good that did. He grasped the flimsy ladder and started to hoist himself up only to find that his legs felt as if they'd turned to jelly, although his arms were as strong as ever. He gritted his teeth and hauled himself by the muscles in his arms alone.

When he reached the top, he looked back over his shoulder to find that Doctor Washington had followed him.

"They don't talk no more," Doctor Washington said, "but if you give me a good price I'll show you the trick of it..."

A door of the other caravan burst open.

"Who's that you're selling your secrets to?" the person called Bertie said. Jack couldn't determine Bertie's gender, only that whoever it was wore a coat that was dark, hooded, and entirely too large.

Jack turned his back to them and peered into the tank. A film of algae coated the sides of the tank and made a blanket over the edge of the water. The water smelled brackish. In another day or two, it might become a full-fledged septic pit. Still, it was water, and somewhere in there was a porpoise, or two.

"Don't mind the dead one," Doctor Washington said. "I've been meaning to get him out of there, sanitation, you know, but the other one won't let me."

The surface rippled, and one glazed eye peered out.

"You can't have him," the porpoise said to Jack.

"But he's my brother," Jack said to the porpoise. "At least, I think he might be. He is Thomas, isn't he?" He realized that speaking to the porpoise took no effort at all, now, as if whatever alchemy lay in his mother's conch shell had penetrated into his very self, or uncovered him to himself, as the case might be.

"You can't make 'em talk like that!" Bertie chortled. "Making funny noises like they do."

The porpoise raised her head out of the water and looked at Jack squarely. "And who are you?"

"Jack."

Behind Jack, Doctor Washington and Bertie had drawn closer. "Seems maybe he can," Doctor Washington said. "You hold out here, Bertie. I'm just stepping inside a moment."

"Sure, I'll keep it in hand," Bertie said.

The porpoise dove back into the pool. A moment later, she nudged Thomas's body to the surface. Jack sat down and let his feet into the water. The itching eased instantly. He reached towards Thomas's wrinkled, dark body. It was not the same smooth grey skin he remembered, but there was something about Thomas's eyes, the shape of his face, that had remained the same even in age and death. Jack slid a little further into the pool.

"Oh, dear," the porpoise said. "You're going to be one of them."

"One of who?"

"The mer-people," the porpoise spat. "No offense to your mother in particular, it's all of them. And it's more the mermaids than the mer-men. You do know that they only make mer-men by magic?

Mermaids are born that way. Insufferable creatures."

"No, I didn't know," Jack said. He reached down to touch Thomas's side, but the female porpoise abruptly pushed the corpse away. The body was bloated, but not yet disintegrating.

"Thomas might not want to contribute to this," she said to Jack with a sniff.

"But who are you?" Jack asked, puzzled at the porpoise's officious manner.

"Thomas's wife. Obviously." She looked at him as if he were a foolish pup, and sank herself and Thomas's body under the surface.

"Bring him back!" Jack called after her.

She popped her head back out. "I won't be long, myself. Nor you," she said. "I will commune with his spirit."

Jack didn't like what she'd said, or the little that he'd understood of it. He was trying to get his head around it, but that was Thomas, there, dead in the water, and what was he, himself? His mother had mentioned making him a tail, but he hadn't given it much thought since. At first he'd been more interested in finding his brothers, then and there had been Miss Parker. He sighed and swished his feet in the water. It did feel better to have them submerged, even in the muck of that tank. He didn't see the two carnival people as they closed in behind him, but he did hear the click of a blade opening.

"Now you just come along," Bertie said.

"We don't want trouble," Doctor Washington added, pulling out a heavy-looking pistol.

From where Jack sat, he could hardly even draw

his sword. He pulled up his aching legs and turned to face them, kneeling awkwardly on the deck, his back to the tank. The carnival men below him held their weapons with expert ease. The sword was only good for show, or perhaps a lucky hit, if it came to that. Jack hoped that it wouldn't.

"I beg your pardon," Jack said, using his best accountancy-student voice, "but I don't want any trouble, either. I am simply looking for the porpoise called Thomas. If you will render his body to me I will take it to its rightful resting place."

"Crazy as a loon," Doctor Washington muttered.

"He wants the dead one?" Bertie said incredulously, almost dropping his knife.

"You can have it if you can get it out of there," Doctor Washington said, setting his foot on the ladder.

Jack attempted to improve his position by heaving himself to a stand, so that he might be capable of wielding his sword. His legs shook under him, as if from exhaustion. He hoped they would hold.

The other porpoise, Thomas's wife, nudged the corpse up behind him. "Here, take him," she said. "He says there's no help for it, if your mother doesn't use his body she'll find another one."

"But I'm already changing," Jack said.

"They need a bit of kindred fish to finish the job, that's what I hear," the porpoise said.

Doctor Washington had reached the platform and stood uncomfortably close to him, gun at the ready. Jack took a panicked swipe with his sword and knocked the showman's hat to the deck. Doctor Washington bent to pick it up, keeping his eye and his pistol trained on Jack the whole time.

"You say you don't want any trouble?" he said as he replaced his hat.

"That's right," Jack said.

"And you want the body of my talking fish?"

Jack nodded. "And this other one, the live one, too."

"I'll sell them to you, then," Doctor Washington said. "For scientifical purposes only. No competing shows. A bargain at twenty pound."

It was a good deal more than Jack had left in his pockets. "I'll agree to no competing shows, but twenty pounds?" He could hardly imagine paying such a price, even if he did have it on hand. Aunt Ermie would be flabbergasted. Aunt Ermie would drive a hard bargain. Jack cleared his throat.

"I rather think you should pay me to do the work of hauling him away for you," Jack said, "and taking the other one to the river before she dies, too."

Bertie guffawed. "You've met your match there, now, Doc."

Doctor Washington ignored his colleague. "You've got your reasons there, I've got mine," he said to Jack. "They're worth a tenner to me, no less."

"Ten?" Jack said, trying to sound shocked. "I'll give you one pound. One pound sterling, said and done."

"And you'll be carrying them yourself?" Doctor Washington asked, eying Jack's figure, which showed no signs of acquaintance with hard labor.

"I'll find a way."

The donkey brayed and resumed kicking its

pail.

"I'll rent you Emma for a shilling," Bertie chimed in.

"She's not yours to rent!" Doctor Washington shouted.

"She's half mine, and you've had more use of her than I have," Bertie complained.

"I'll have my fee from it, too," said Doctor Washington, turning to point his pistol at his fellow showman.

"If you'd pay your half her feed, I'd consider it," Bertie said.

"I have been paying!"

"Have not!"

The two carnival showmen began a heated accounting of the donkey's various expenses and profitable uses, holstering their firearms and producing canes from their hip pockets. They waved the canes wildly in each others' general direction, but never hit their marks. Jack squatted back down by the tank.

"Can you get yourself out of there?" he asked the living porpoise.

"Nearly," she said, "but you'd best take Thomas first."

"I hope to take you both at once," Jack said, "with the donkey."

The porpoise snorted. "She's barely able to pull the cart with a man in it, let alone the three of us."

"Three of us?"

"You won't be walking far on those." The porpoise nudged Jack's feet, and he felt them loose their firmness at her touch, like the bones inside had turned to melting ice.

"Don't do that!" Jack said. His feet would have to stand him long enough to get the porpoises to the river.

The porpoise curled protectively around Thomas's body, which let out slow bubbles of air as it sank to the bottom of the tub.

"You can't trust a mermaid," the porpoise said. "You know they lay eggs. It's not natural. I always said so, even before I married Thomas and met your mother."

Jack felt that he ought to defend his mother, but he barely knew her. He didn't know where to begin. His brother sank out of sight.

"Hurry now," the porpoise said. "They'll never let you out of this fairground if they see your feet."

Jack's feet were definitely wobbling. He didn't dare pull up his trouser cuffs to look at them.

"And you'll be caught halfway between forms, and that's no good for anyone," the porpoise said.

Jack turned away from the tank. A small crowd had gathered. Bertie stood at the front with the donkey in a rope harness beside him. A boy was bringing a wooden cart around, and the inhabitants of the nearby caravans stood about, gawking.

"You can't be coming in here when we're closed for the night," one of them said. He held a painted cudgel.

"We don't take to vagrants," a woman chimed in. She looked like she needed a fresh coat of paint.

"Or swimmers," said another, who slung a heavy rope over one shoulder.

"Now there," Doctor Washington said, "where's my pound?" The pistol re-appeared, and he was pointing it at Jack again.

Jack dug in his pockets, hoping that carnival people wouldn't notice what was happening to his legs.

§

CHAPTER FOUR: ENGAGEMENTS

The bargain's off," said someone. Jack looked up to see Miss Iris Parker walk in as if she were constable of the fairgrounds.

"Miss..." Jack began, but Iris glared at him and he took the hint. It didn't take much to silence him. He needed all his breath to keep from falling into the tank with Thomas's widow. Jack sat back down and dangled his legs into the water, feeling the tension rush out of his ankles only to be replaced by a disquieting, gelatinous feeling. Meanwhile, the carnival folk turned away from him to contend with Miss Parker.

"Ladies and... gentlemen," Iris said, very much implying that those were not the terms she would have preferred. "I am an inspector from the Royal Society for the Prevention of Cruelty to Animals. Please. Please show me your animals." The carnival folk started to scatter at the word "inspector," and by the time she finished speaking they were all gone except for Bertie and Doctor Washington, who still had an interest in the porpoises and their promised moneys. Iris took hold of the donkey's harness.

"Oh, you poor thing!" she said to the donkey. She looked daggers at the two remaining carnival men.

"All right," Jack whispered to the porpoise, "Thomas first."

The porpoise dove down and came up carrying Thomas's body across her back. Jack took it beneath the fins and heaved. Agony shot down his legs. Thomas's body slithered through his hands and disintegrated as it hit the water, falling into pieces, almost melting into the murky pool. Jack and Thomas's porpoise-wife watched the remains of his body swirl down into the soupy water. Jack felt that he might faint, but at least he had not cried out. The pain was too unfamiliar, too strange to merit a mere scream. In his pocket, the conch shell seemed to shrink.

"And marine animals!" Iris was saying to the carnival men. "Really, you ought to know that there's a license required, and these conditions!" she sniffed the air and glared at Jack. "Sir," she said to him, "will you assist me?"

"He is one of your lot, then," Bertie said.

"I thought he might be," Doctor Washington grumbled.

"So I am," Jack said, quickly. "I would help, but I only just... I seem to have injured my shoulder. Would you gentlemen help me bring the living porpoise into the cart?"

Whether it was Iris's air of authority or the fact that the carnival men really did want to get rid of their no-longer-talking porpoise, they shrugged and lent their shoulders to the effort of putting the porpoise into the cart. Iris distracted them just enough that Jack managed to hide his feet from them.

"Never mind Thomas's body," the porpoise-wife said to Jack as the carnival men hefted her body out of the tank. "His spirit is at rest. As much as it can be, with all this mer-witchery going on."

"Are you sure?" Jack said.

Again, she looked at him like he were a child. "Why would I say so, otherwise? Really."

Iris looked at Jack. She took one look at the change that was coming over his legs, and stifled a gasp. "Are you all right, sir?" she asked.

"I seem to have injured my back," Jack said loudly. "Do you think I might ride in the cart as well?"

"We won't be able to get the other porpoise, then," Iris said.

"It's all right," Jack said. "There's really not enough left of him to bring."

Emma the donkey brayed and kicked.

"Well," Iris said, "I hate to burden this poor creature, but..."

"She'll pull for you, she will," Bertie chimed in, giving the donkey a slap on the rump, "only give us a shilling for losing her."

Iris looked at Bertie with disgust, but dug in her purse and tossed him a coin.

"Hey, that's mine!" Doctor Washington said,

making a grab for the coin.

"Isn't," said Bertie.

Jack slid down from the stage around the tank and limped to the cart as quickly as he could. He pulled his lower body in as far as it would go. Thomas's wife felt strangely warm beside him. There was a flea-ridden blanket which he pulled up over his changing extremities.

"Shall we go?" Iris asked, worried.

"Yes!" Jack said. "Please. With all haste."

"Give it here!" Doctor Washington shouted at Bertie.

"Not on your life!" Bertie shouted back, waving his cane. Iris tugged on the donkey's harness.

"Well I'll get my own shilling off them, then," Doctor Washington said, menacing.

Iris pulled harder and the donkey shifted.

"See here," Doctor Washington said, approaching them. "My colleague has a mistaken notion that all of this is his," he said, indicating the donkey and cart.

Iris continued to urge the donkey forward. "You didn't deny that he owned a share of the donkey," she said.

"No," he said, "but the cart's mine, and you'll compensate me for the use of it. And the blanket. I'll have that blanket back."

Jack clutched the blanket tighter as Doctor Washington approached.

"What are you, chilled?" he said to Jack. "Or hiding something?" He strode over and yanked the blanket away, with Jack still holding one corner tightly.

Jack froze, then pulled the blanket back over

himself. Iris heaved a deep sigh. Doctor Washington took one wide-eyed look at Jack's transforming limbs and whistled.

"Here! Here!" Doctor Washington shouted. "A real freak for the show!" The carnival people, who had so recently scattered at Iris's approach, leaped out of their hiding places, brandishing blades and laughing, or so it seemed to Jack.

"I wish you hadn't done that," Iris muttered. She drew a pistol out from the folds of her skirt and fired.

The donkey bolted. Doctor Washington fired, too, narrowly missing Iris. The donkey slowed, but then Bertie charged after them. The donkey broke into a panicked canter, slipping the reins out of Iris's hands. She fired back at the carnival men. A shout let Jack know that she had hit her mark, but he couldn't look, it was all he could do to stay in the cart. He clutched on for dear life, trying to keep the porpoise from sliding out, too. They careened through the fairgrounds to the front gate. Iris shot the lock open with her pistol then pointed her gun at an adolescent boy who had sped ahead of the others, unarmed.

"Open it," she ordered.

He did so, and Iris fired a final shot at the approaching crowd of carnies. They skidded to a stop at the gate, as if held back by some kind of magical wall.

Doctor Washington alone took one step outside. "He had a tail!" he said, clutching a handkerchief to his bleeding shoulder.

"He didn't," Bertie said. "Who do you think we are, easy marks?"

That drew a chuckle, but Jack and Iris were already far enough away that they couldn't hear what followed.

As they reached a main road, the donkey slowed and Iris, still looking warily over her shoulder, hid the gun again. At the next corner, she led the cart into a small alley and looked at Jack quizzically.

"Is something the matter?" she asked him.

"I don't know exactly," Jack said, "but I'm very happy you came along just then. I wouldn't have been able to manage."

Iris snorted. "I should think not."

"And I think something's happening to my legs."

"It certainly looks like that, but what? I've never seen anything like this." She dropped the donkey's harness and came around the back of the cart. When she picked up the blanket, the porpoise hissed. That startled the donkey, who backed up abruptly. Iris jumped aside to avoid getting run over by the cart.

"Tell her to get her hands off," the porpoise hissed at Jack.

"I don't mind her," Jack said.

"Well, I do," said the porpoise.

"I guess we'd better keep going," Jack said to Iris. "I'd show you, but the porpoise has objections, apparently. Maybe we should get to the river first."

"What did she say?" Iris asked.

"To keep your hands off," Jack said with a shrug. He paused. "You don't find it strange that..." He wasn't sure where to start. "That I can talk to her, and things?"

"There are many strange things, and people, in

the world," Iris said levelly.

"But, I mean..."

"I'm a showman's daughter on one side, and part selkie on the other side," she said.

"Part selkie? Really?" Jack asked.

Iris nodded. She looked over her shoulder to make sure that they were still alone, then let her shawl drop slightly at her neck. "I only have a little patch, here. Mother said it was just like what her mother had. Not that she saw her often. She went back to the sea, or at least that's what they say."

Jack reached to touch it, but the porpoise hissed and struck his arm with a hard flipper punch. She eyed Iris skeptically.

"She's not one of them," Thomas's widow said.

"But you can understand her even so?" Jack asked the porpoise.

"Only a little bit," the porpoise conceded.

"I suppose we'd better keep going," Iris said, reluctantly leaving the blanket untouched. She took the donkey's lead rope again and started forward.

The donkey refused to budge. The sick feeling in Jack's stomach threatened to overwhelm him. Nearby, a bakery opened its shutters, sending the aroma of fresh-baked rolls out into the morning mist. The donkey pulled towards it, nearly unseating Jack and causing the porpoise to roll onto his lower limbs... or limb, as the case might be. He pushed her off.

"You're still too bony down there," the porpoise said, disapprovingly.

"I don't see how it makes any difference to you," Jack said.

"You don't see much, do you?"

Iris was looking at the donkey. "Do you suppose she wants breakfast?"

Jack's stomach churned. With all the bizarre and discomfiting sensations in what used to be his legs, he'd hardly thought of how little he'd eaten in the past day and a half. A few hot rolls would do him good. Besides, if he were to be a merman he probably wouldn't have much chance to get fresh-baked rolls. The thought saddened him.

"I certainly would," Jack said. "Like to have breakfast, that is."

Iris shook her head. "But I don't have any money. I spent it all on the ferry."

Jack straightened in his seat, ignoring the porpoise's grumblings. "I have plenty," he said. "Plenty enough for rolls, in any case. Here." He fished out his money and handed it all to Iris.

"Will you be all right?" she asked.

Jack nodded, and Iris went inside. The donkey lumbered closer to the bakery door. The porpoise growled and turned away from Jack, sulking.

"We're on our way back to the river," Jack said, hoping that would cheer the porpoise.

"Yes, where there are plenty of good fish for breakfast. You don't want those things, do you?"

"I certainly prefer them to fish," Jack said. Did the porpoise really expect him to eat fish, his near kinfolk?

"Finicky," the porpoise said, "just like your brother."

Jack was relieved to hear that Thomas had at least shared this with him, though he wondered how he'd survived as a porpoise. Did they eat anything other than fish?

"I won't have it," the porpoise continued. "Besides I don't like you giving your money to that woman, quarter-selkie or not."

Jack was about to ask the porpoise why it meant anything to her who he gave his money to, when Iris emerged with a large basket of baked goods. "I couldn't have spent all that money if I'd tried!" she said. "I didn't know you were rich!"

"I'm not," Jack said as reached for a roll. "That's all the money I have in the world."

Iris blushed. "I suppose I shouldn't have spent so much of it, then."

"It doesn't matter," Jack said. He sank his teeth into the roll as Iris offered the donkey one, and then dangled another in front of her, which inspired her to a trot despite the heavy weight in her cart. Jack held onto the sides. He would have liked a bit of tea to wash breakfast down, but he needed to reach the river more urgently. The porpoise's mood did not improve as the cart rumbled through the waking town, but after a while the motion lulled her into a fitful doze.

They had nearly reached the promenade by the time he'd worked up the courage to talk to Iris again.

"You're not really with the RSPCA, are you?" Jack asked.

"Not at the moment," Iris said, "but I have been. It's one of my... arguments with my father. He doesn't approve."

"No, I don't suppose he would," Jack said. "Why did you follow me... or, come to rescue me?"

Iris rolled her eyes. "Father said that he wanted his sword back."

"Oh, dear," Jack said. "But you said that it was yours?"

"It is," Iris said.

"I must thank you for it," Jack said. "It came in quite handy. People seemed to respect me more."

"I'm glad to hear it," Iris said. She walked a few paces more, looking for a convenient way down to the water's edge. "My grandmother... well, as soon as I saw you talk to that porpoise, even before that, there was something in my blood that..." She blushed. "I don't usually tell people about this. They'd think I was lying."

"There's a great deal I've never even thought about," Jack said, "because my aunt would have beat me for spinning tales if I talked about it. Aunt Ermie said that my mother left me in a basket. I just took her word for it."

"But where did she leave you?"

"With my father." Jack stopped. "I never thought of that. How would anyone get to the lighthouse, except by sea?" He sighed. "I suppose it doesn't matter now. She came to meet me, just before I met you. She's a mermaid, of all things."

A spasm ripped through Jack's ankles, or what was left of them, and he cried out. Iris rushed around to the cart. She held his hands in hers, and gazed into his eyes. Her eyes were a deep, soft brown. He forgot his pain, for a moment.

"You'll understand, then," she said. "The sword was my grandfather's, my selkie-grandmother's husband. Father always said it was because of her blood that my mother left when I was so young. He said the selkie blood made her unreliable, as if *he* were some paragon of stability."

"I think you'll need to take my shoes off," Jack said as the feeling came back into his lower extremities.

Iris lifted the blanket and her jaw dropped. "What are you?" she said.

The porpoise stirred, then sank into a deeper slumber.

"I don't know, just that my mother was a mermaid."

"Wouldn't that make you a merman?"

"Well, no. I mean, not until now."

Iris frowned. "I don't think that mermaids and selkies get along very well."

"I don't mind," Jack said. "In fact the porpoise here said not to trust mermaids, even though my mother is one. She said mermaids are just born that way, but that mermen are made. I guess that's what's happening to me."

"So you wouldn't mind that I might put on a seal skin some day?"

Jack gritted his teeth and looked down at where his shoes had been protruding from the blanket a moment before. A fin peeped out, and though it had the vestiges of toes at the end of its spines, they were melting like ice. He could still feel a little space between his legs, but when he tried to pull his knees apart they wouldn't budge. He peeked under the blanket. His trousers had somehow gotten torn along their inner seams.

"I think I'd rather prefer if you did slip on a seal skin," Jack said. "Then you could come live in the sea with me."

"Will you really go into the sea, then?" Iris asked mournfully.

"I don't know that I have a choice any more," Jack said, "My mother warned me. If I could have gotten there before Thomas died, then maybe I could have stayed on land, because he would be with her in the sea. That was her reason, anyway. I'm the only one left, so she said I had to go back."

"But what could you have done?" Iris asked, prodding the donkey forward again.

"I don't know," Jack said. "I never could have saved him, he must have been sick when they caught him, if this wife of his was caught at the same time. She isn't even as sick as the poor creature your father had. I wouldn't have found him at all if I hadn't met you, and I wouldn't have been able to get to him much faster, even if I'd known where he was from the outset."

"So you'll be a merman, of all things," Iris mused.

"I'm not very well suited to life on land, so maybe it's just as well?"

"I'm not well-suited to it, either," Iris said, "but I'd hoped that... Oh, never mind."

She turned away again to urge the donkey forwards. Jack heard her sniff, and then she raised her hand to wipe her nose on her sleeve. "I'd hoped that we could have built a different kind of life," she said, swallowing her tears. "I'm sure we could have, but now..." She glanced back at Jack's legs and shook her head. "Father will outright murder me if I let you go."

"He wouldn't," Jack said. "Besides, you have the sword, now."

"No, you'd better take it," she said, "in case you need it, with the other mermen. They're bound to be fearsome fighters, that's what all the stories say." She led the donkey towards a muddy stretch of riverbank.

"I don't really know anything about mermen," Jack said, "and even this porpoise thinks I'm a fool." He certainly didn't know what it would mean to *be* a merman. "What I do know is that you're by far the most charming young lady I've ever met, and..."

The donkey slid to a stop. She did not like the mud. Iris gave one stiff tug on her rope, and when the donkey refused to budge, Iris dropped the lead and went to Jack. The porpoise stirred in her sleep.

"I don't think anyone's ever called me charming before," Iris said. "Not in earnest, anyway."

"I was wondering if..." Jack said. Then he stopped to eye the expanse of mud between himself and his future habitat. It wasn't such a long stretch. He could drag himself, if he had to, and so could the porpoise.

"You said earlier," he started again, "about making another sort of life for ourselves."

Iris blushed. "It was just a girlish fancy."

"But you see, I had thoughts like that too, and I thought maybe, that is, I wondered..."

The donkey slid forward, waking the porpoise, and tumbling Jack onto the mud. He fell on his back. Iris bent over him, revealing more bosom than he'd seen in... well, almost ever. Not including his mother, but that wasn't the same, besides which she was a mermaid. This was a lady.

Lying on his back, he said: "Would you do me the honor, make me a happy man, I mean, be my wife?"

Iris's eyes lit up. "I would!" she said. "Father's been after me to think of that kind of thing lately, since I turned sixteen, but I just couldn't, not until yesterday, when I met you, and..."

The porpoise shrieked.

"You can't!" the porpoise said, baring her teeth. "He's mine!"

Jack looked at the porpoise dumbfounded as she flopped herself towards him, glaring at Iris.

"But I say she can!" Jack said.

"And I say she can't," the porpoise replied. "You're promised to me, by the law of the sea, as my deceased husband's brother. It is your duty to marry me."

Iris looked puzzled.

The porpoise took a mouthful of his jacket and tugged him towards the river. Jack grabbed at the mud with his hands.

It was still early in the morning, but the few passers by walking along the promenade stopped to stare.

Jack turned to argue with the porpoise, while fighting to get himself out of her grip. "Well, that may be the law of the sea," he said, "but we're not in the sea. We're on land. And here, marrying your brother's widow is against the law entirely."

The porpoise glared, and let him go.

"Besides," Jack said, "I choose to marry this woman, if she'll have me."

"We'll see about that!" the porpoise grumbled. With that, she pushed and sidled herself away down the river bank until she plopped into the water.

The passers-by were starting to slow down and

peer at Jack with interest. Iris threw the blanket back over his tail.

A searing pain ratcheted through Jack's bones. He gasped.

"I think I'd better get to the river, too," he said. "I'm so very sorry I can't stay. I'd love to, you know."

Iris bit her lip and lifted him up onto what had been his knees. She helped him slide down to the water's edge. The tide had begun to turn, and the river ran swiftly out toward the channel.

With his new fin touching the water, Jack felt instant relief. He looked up at Iris again.

"I do mean it," he said. "I want to marry you, but I don't know how we'll manage it. You'll have to go back to Plymouth and send a message to my father. He's the keeper of the Eddystone Light. I'll come find you."

"I'll find you, too," she promised. "I think I can do it. Maybe I can even find an old seal-skin somewhere."

A new sound came towards him from the river, something which pulled him in deeper, almost against his will. It was a sweet sound, and he would have thought it all that he ever wanted to hear... except for Iris's voice.

Iris looked out beyond him and frowned. "I think they're coming for you, the mermaids. I'm glad I gave you that sword, in case you need it to fend off other suitors, besides myself and that porpoise."

Even from the shore, he could see the mermaids licking their lips at the sight of him. They were calling to him. "I think I have to go," he said. "I can't live on land like this. But I'll tell the mermaids I'm promised to you, and they'll have to take that for an answer."

"Yes, they will," Iris said. She looked over her shoulder. Some of the people walking on the promenade had started to edge towards them across the mud. "He's fine," she shouted to them. "Just going for a morning swim!"

They slowed their approach enough for her to lean down and give Jack a parting kiss. It was pure bliss. Jack had never felt so alive.

"I must get back to you!" he said. "Tell your father that you're marrying an accountant, or an accountancy student, anyway. That's nearly as good!" Behind him, the mermaids hissed.

"That's lovely," Iris said, looking worried. She touched his hand as he slipped away with the tide. "I'll see you at Plymouth! Just as soon as I can!"

Up on the shore a boy from the carnival reclaimed the donkey, and the passers-by went about their business.

§

Iris trudged off to the ferry while Jack slipped away to sea. He didn't want to go, but the pain in his legs – or what was left of them – was so intense that he could barely stay afloat.

"I'll see you soon," Jack shouted back to Iris, but she was already too far away to hear.

A horn sounded, a deafening boom, practically on top of him. Startled, Jack looked up to find a massive steamer bearing down. He dove under the churning behemoth. When he surfaced again, he was half a mile out from shore and just as far down-river. Iris was long out of sight.

"Sss," said someone near him. "Pretty words, new merman."

Jack flopped around until he found the speaker, who tittered at his clumsy efforts to control his new tail. That was all right, he was used to people snickering at him. He brushed the water out of his eyes and looked around.

A dozen young mermaids circled him. Their hair color ranged from jet-black to white-blonde, and their skin was every shade from nut brown to seafoam. Their eyes were fishy, much fishier than his own, but it gave them a wide-eyed look, which might have been quite pretty if he hadn't been comparing them to Iris.

"I think he looks quite nice," said one of them, a brunette who wore a jade-and-seaflower necklace draped over her bare bosoms.

"If it weren't for those *clothes*," said another, a slightly older, blonde.

"Shall we help you with them?" offered a third, smiling with her brightly painted lips.

"We would so like to see..."

The mermaids collapsed into fits of giggles.

Jack cleared his throat.

"I'll see to my own clothes, thank you very much," he said.

They giggled again. "Come with us," said the largest mermaid in the group. She had black hair, ivory skin, and wore thick gold bangles in her ears. "We'll show you a few things. We'll have those clothes off you yet!"

"It's really quite all right," Jack said. Then he

yawned.

"Poor baby, he's tired," said one of the mermaids mockingly.

"They always are, you know," said the large mermaid. "We'll carry him along, then."

Jack's efforts to wave them away were too sleepy to have much effect. He kept a grip on his sword as they shouldered in around him, rubbing up against him in the cool waters and carrying him until he fell asleep.

§

When Jack woke again, the pain in his legs – or rather, his tail – was gone, and his mother lounged beside him on a bit of tidal sand, cracking open an oyster. She slurped the meat down, inspected the shell for pearls, then tossed it into the waves. Jack was struck again by how young she looked, or at least well-preserved. She must have been at least forty, and was probably a good deal older to judge by the look in her eyes.

"We meet again," she said. "I can't say I like your recent behavior."

"What recent behavior?" Jack said. "I've been asleep! Where am I?"

"You know what I'm talking about," she said. "We have a desperate shortage of mermen here, and the girls are beside themselves over your unthinking declaration to that bluestocking on the shore."

"She's not a bluestocking! Goodness!" Jack exclaimed. "Well, maybe she is a bit, but what does the shortage of mermen have to do with it?"

His mother waved her hand. "I don't need to explain *that* to you, do I? Surely you learned *something* on land."

"Not much, not that kind of thing," he said. "Aunt Ermie saw to it that I had a respectable upbringing. I'm going to be – or was going to be – an accountant. I don't suppose I can go back to school like this."

"No," his mother said. "Is this Aunt Ermie the female relation your father was always talking about? The one who didn't approve of me?"

"Didn't believe in you, more like," Jack said.

Jack looked down at his tail. The mermaids had taken most of his clothes as he slept, but they'd left him his belt and the sword. His tail was long, at least twice as long as his legs had been, and it was green-blue like deep water in a shaded cove. The scales turned golden and then pale as they merged with his skin, which thankfully looked more or less the same. He didn't like having his torso bare, but at least it was recognizably his own.

"You'll have to work a bit on those arms to swim any distance," his mother said disapprovingly. "I won't have you being the scrawniest merman in the sea, even if you made foolish promises to a land girl."

The voice of Jack's father echoed in his mind: "*Son, I want you to marry a land girl,*" he'd said. "*A nice land girl.*"

"I don't see that my declaration was all that foolish," Jack said.

His mother just laughed and opened another oyster.

"Would you like one?" she finally said.

Jack realized that he was, in fact, quite hungry. "Well yes, I would."

"Here." She tossed him one, whole.

He had no notion of how to open it. "Is there anything else?"

She looked at him a long moment before answering his unspoken question. "You just *tell it* to open. Then bite it out with your teeth, like this," she demonstrated. "Even your father knows that."

Jack really was hungry, so he tried it, barbaric as it looked. It seemed to work. He slurped the oyster down, then ate two more.

"Why do they listen?" he wondered out loud.

"You, my dear, have a great deal to learn," his mother said. "Everyone in the sea listens to the mer-people. Except the dolphins sometimes, and the selkies, of course. They don't listen to anyone, not even each other."

"I see," Jack said.

His mother shrugged and tossed him another oyster.

§

Jack fell asleep again. Despite being half-submerged in water and wearing hardly a stitch, he didn't feel cold. He dreamed of Iris, the swirl of her skirts as she pulled out the gun, the spark in her eyes as she handed him the blade, and the way she brushed her hair back as she leaned down over him. He dreamed of her hands playing on his chest, running down towards his...

His eyes snapped open. Iris was gone. In her place were the mermaids who had hauled him away from her. They had slithered up out of the sea and circled him while his mother reclined nearby, ignoring the goings-on.

Jack pushed himself up. "Go away!" he said.

They tittered and retreated a few inches. The pale blonde batted her eyelashes at him. He tried to turn away, only to be confronted with the large, black-haired one. She shook her gold hoop earrings at him.

"Can't you get me something better than these, husband?" she said.

"Husband?" Jack said. "What?" He looked around. The mermaids were all nodding. His mother looked over at them lazily.

"Now girls," she said, "I told you to let him rest."

"But he's so..." one of them started, then they all giggled.

"She called me husband!" Jack said, pointing at the large one.

"Well of course," said his mother, swimming over. "Why wouldn't she? We made you a merman for these mermaids. They want to be mer-women, and not just with sailors."

"Besides, sailors are so hard to come by these days," said a honey-colored blonde, "not like it used to be when so many men were 'pressed into the navy. *Those* sailors practically leaped overboard at a wink and a whistle."

"Oh, as if you're old enough to remember," said a redhead who Jack hadn't noticed before. He tried to count them, but they kept swimming around, weaving in and out behind each other. There had to be at least dozen of them.

"But I don't even know who you are, any of you!" Jack protested.

"You hardly knew that girl on the shore either, did you?" his mother said. "You didn't have any such attachments when I met you the other night."

Jack narrowed his eyes. "How do you know?"

"We can tell," his mother said. "We just can. It's how we capture our men."

"Well, I don't much like being captured," Jack said.

"You didn't much like life on land, either," his mother retorted. "I think we can offer a pleasing alternative."

"Well, that was before... before I met Miss Parker. Besides, there were compensations."

"Compensations? We can give you compensations." The young mermaids tightened their circle around him and began to massage various parts of his body, which responded with a warmth Jack would have rather suppressed.

"There he rises!" said one of them.

"Again," said another.

"Off! Get off of me, all of you! I am not your husband!"

"But we say you are..."

"Shh," his mother said. "We'll have him agree yet."

"This can't be legal," Jack muttered. That sparked another round of amusement for the mermaids. "Well, it can't be. I haven't agreed to it."

His mother sighed. "It's only a matter of time, dear. They will be very persuasive."

"Well I don't want to be persuaded by them. Besides, I'm promised elsewhere."

The mermaids collectively rolled their eyes. "We'll have to take this to the king," the large one said.

"Oh, the king, the king!" they exclaimed. "I love the king." Their circling took on a giddy frenzy. They laughed and petted each other and licked their lips.

"Well marry him, then!" Jack said.

"He has a hundred wives already," his mother said. "Besides, he's too old for these girls."

"Is he?" Jack said.

His mother shrugged.

"But not too old for you?"

The mermaids giggled yet again.

"Stop it!" Jack shouted. "And yes, I think you'd better take me to this king of yours."

"Yes, husband," they said, swimming in a circle around him, rather like sharks.

§

They swam towards their king's court for two full days, during which the mermaids, one after the other, attempted to seduce Jack with wiles which frankly bewildered him. He had certainly never experienced anything like it on shore. It was exactly the opposite of his life experience up until a few days ago, and it was all a bit too much. He told them so, but they laughed and continued to rub themselves against him. One even laid an egg, to show him that she could do it. A nice, snug opening appeared in her tail.

"That's where you... you know," she said. "I bet we can make it nearly as big around as an egg."

"I'm sure we can," said another.

"Just stop it!" said Jack. He even fantasized about using his sword to drive them off, but his mother had assured him that she wouldn't let things get too far out of hand. She did seem to have some authority over the "girls."

In between their attempts to seduce Jack, the mermaids told him about how splendid the king and his court were, so that by the time Jack arrived he was prepared to be disappointed. He was not.

The court was a shoal near the Isle of Wight, decorated with shells, stones, and corals from as far away as Africa and South America. The light bouncing off the water formed an arch near the king, which danced with spray from the rocks. The mermaids swam into the court in single file, as solemn as mermaids could be. Shellfish of every description were served on platters borne up by ships' figureheads, and seaweed salads lay damp and sparkling in giant shells. The king sunned himself on a sandy stretch, surrounded by some of his wives. He looked authoritative, ready to defend his people, and perhaps the slightest bit spoiled. He had a bushy beard and wore a gold-trimmed captain's uniform as well as a crown made out of dangerous-looking pointed shells.

Jack eyed the mer-king's sword, a broad, well-traveled blade. The king's arms matched his weapon – well-muscled from shoulder to wrist, with a prominent white scar just over the left elbow. Jack looked around for some place to leave his sword. He had no desire to test his blade against the king's.

"Go on!" his mother urged, impatient.

Jack gave up looking for a sword-rack and crept forward, dragging his sword behind him.

The king scrutinized Jack as he approached. Jack made a clumsy attempt at a bow. His tail got in the way. The mer-king laughed. Jack paled.

"Welcome!" The king said. "We can always use a new merman, especially one that comes bearing his own sword. Thank you, Marissa," he said.

Jack exhaled. His mother was blushing. Marissa. So that was her name!

"You may go to my chamber," he said to her.

The young mermaids oohed and aahed as the king placed a lingering kiss on Marissa's eager mouth. Jack felt... embarrassed.

"And now may we bed our husband?" the large mermaid said impatiently.

"What?" the king boomed. "You haven't already? You've been remiss in your duties."

"We haven't been!" said the very pale one. "But he has!" she pointed a long finger at Jack. The mermaid king tapped his fingers together. "Marissa," he said, "come back here and explain this to me."

Jack's mother reluctantly reversed her course and came to Jack's side. "He developed an attachment," she said bitterly.

"Attachments can be severed, you know," the king said to Jack.

"But what if I don't want to?" Jack asked.

"Why not?" said the king. "Look at what you can have here!"

In the sunlight, the watery opulence of the

mermaids' court looked like a small paradise, but Jack still felt ill at ease.

"Where are the other mermen?" he asked.

"Other mermen?" the king asked. "Oh dear, you're not..."

"No! Not at all," Jack said. "I just feel that there isn't anyone like me here, just as there wasn't anyone like me on shore."

"That's what it's always like for boys, though," his mother said.

"So, where are they?" Jack asked the king.

The king shrugged. "Oh, hither and yon. I have no rule over them."

"Then you have no rule over me, either."

The king sighed. "Wait here," he said to the mermaids. "The new merman and I will have a talk. Man to man, as it were." One of the mermaids handed the king his sword, with a lascivious look in her eye. He patted her on the rump and swam over to Jack.

"Now, what seems to be the problem?" the king asked as they swam away.

"Well, firstly that these mermaids think that I'm their husband, though I haven't said I would be."

"That's how they are. After so many love-lorn years at sea, who can say no? I was captain of a four-masted schooner, but when we wrecked and I had the choice between all these beauties and near-certain death, I dove right in. I've never much looked back, nor do most mermen. It's a bit painful, growing a tail, but you should be feeling better by now. Managing it all right?"

"It feels fine, actually, and my swimming has improved quite a bit in the last few days."

"Good, good. So you should be in the mood for some female attentions."

"I..." Jack had to collect his thoughts. "I am," he said. "Actually, I think I am in the mood, just not with these females. I'm in love."

The mermaid king let out a resonant guffaw, then wiped away his tears of laughter. "Really?" he said. "I never heard of such a thing. The girls are usually very good at..."

"And besides," Jack cut in, "I miss coffee, and mince pies, and things like that."

The king nodded. "What I wouldn't do for a good roast and some Yorkshire pudding. We can get the claret to wash it down with, but the salt tack in shipwrecks just isn't the same."

"No, I imagine it isn't," Jack said. "Not that I have anything against oysters. They're fine, but..."

"The diet is a little wearying at first," said the king, "but you get used to it, and I'm sure I'm healthier than I ever was before I came here. I do miss land food sometimes, especially around Christmas. A raw lobster just isn't the same as a good roast goose."

Jack propelled himself forward. He couldn't pace on a tail, but he could manage something like it. He looked back at the court to see a few mermaids – his mermaids, he supposed – looking out after them while the rest dribbled seaweed into their mouths.

"So do I have to marry them?" Jack asked the king.

"I can't command you to, but I think you're a fool for letting them go."

"Well, I don't mind being called a fool," Jack

said. "I'm used to worse insults. Shall we make a bargain?"

"What kind of bargain?" the king asked.

"You tell them to stay here while I swim back to Plymouth, and I'll bring you a roast for Christmas dinner. If my fiancée will still have me, I'll marry her. If not, well..." Jack didn't really want to think about that. He hoped that Iris would still have him.

"I never thought I'd brighten at the thought of cold mutton, but it does sound a long sight better than another lobster at Christmas. I accept your offer, young man. Good luck to you, and this girl of yours!"

§

CHAPTER FIVE: JACK AT SEA

Jack swam back to the shoal, filled up on oysters, and said a quick farewell to the mermaids. He couldn't stomach the colorful but slimy seaweed salads which they seemed to enjoy. The mermaid king took his provisions like medicine, then romped off to enjoy a bout with Jack's mother. Jack found it all quite distasteful. While his mother was closeted with the king, Jack set out for Plymouth.

Since his transformation, he'd been surrounded by mermaids at every moment, asleep or awake, so much so that he'd hardly seen what the ocean was like. The depths weren't as dark as he would have expected, or perhaps his eyes had adjusted to the gloom. In any case, he found it quite easy to navigate, and his tail carried him through the water at a swift clip. The speed of it was really quite thrilling. He could keep pace with most of the boats on the channel, and swam through the daylight hours without tiring too much.

The first days of his swim were uneventful, except for a brief scare when a large shark crossed his path. On the second morning he discovered a shipwreck and dove down to investigate. He found a cache of gold jewelry in an antique, seaweed-covered box. Whoever had once owned it was long dead, and it seemed a great waste to leave it there. The fish certainly didn't care about it. With only a passing twinge of guilt, Jack took it with him.

On the afternoon of the third day he found himself near Plymouth. Myriad signs and hints, things he never would have perceived before, told him that he was approaching the town. His fish tail had brought with it the senses of the mermaids. He could see the colors of the water in layers and pattens. He could smell the river water, mingling with the sea, and the different seaweeds and shellfish, all the things mer-people ate. He could hear the swoosh of boats cutting through the waves, the bubbling stirrings of creatures on the sea floor, and the ping-ping of porpoise chatter as he approached the river.

Jack skirted in towards shore to look at the town which had been his childhood home. He'd seen it often enough from the boat that this vantage point was familiar to him, but the house on Sydney Street lay over a hill. He would never go there again, never see his small collection of books, his boyhood bedroom, or Aunt Ermie's impeccable kitchen. He would miss them. He ought to have said goodbye, but he'd given no thought to all that in the search for his brothers, and in finding Iris. He believed that it would all work out if he saw Iris again. He knew that it would.

"Duck, you idiot!"

Jack had been so lost in his reverie that he hadn't noticed the approaching boat. He dove. He didn't have time to wonder who had spoken until he opened his eyes again in the depths, nose to nose with Thomas's porpoise widow.

"Running away from the mermaids, too?" she said. "Who in the sea will you ally yourself with, then?" About twenty other porpoises massed behind her, all wearing the same expression of sneering displeasure. They bore a striking family resemblance to one another.

"I don't see how it's any of your business," Jack said.

"I've explained already. We've come to take you up to my home river. I've rights to you, you know."

"And I've explained already that you don't. I'm not a porpoise. I'm not bound by your laws."

"We'll see about that," she said. Her relations mumbled their support, as much as porpoises can mumble.

Jack wondered if he could out-swim them. He would have liked to try, but they'd circled him in all directions. None of them were much bigger than he was, in fact most of them were a bit smaller. He drew his sword and they retreated a half-stroke. He would never be able to fight his way through all of their sharp teeth and determined fins, and in any case he didn't like the thought of shedding porpoise blood, sharks or no.

"I really have no business with you," Jack said.

"She says you do," said the largest of the

relations, a dark and fearsome looking porpoise. He had a fish-hook sunk into his forehead, grown there and turned into something of an ornament.

"And I say I don't," Jack squeaked. He swam up to the surface to take a breath, and the porpoises followed him.

"We'll take it to our clan chief," said the fish-hook porpoise once they were back underwater. "There'll be war."

Thomas's widow looked worried. "But if the mermaids don't want him..." she began.

Her kinfolk rounded on her. "Since when? You didn't tell us this!"

"I didn't know it!" she said. "But look at him here. He doesn't even have one mermaid bride."

The porpoises mumbled to one another, squinting at Jack.

"That's right," Jack declared. "I don't have a single mermaid wife. I told the mermaid king that I didn't want them, and he washed his hands of it. He said he had no rule over me."

"Is that so?" said the one with the fishhook.

"It is," Jack said.

Thomas's widow huffed. "I never heard such nonsense," she said.

The other porpoises retreated to hold council in a flurry of clicks and whistles faster than Jack could decipher. His would-be wife came nose to nose with him and looked him in the eye, showing all her teeth. Jack's hand went to his sword-hilt.

"I never would have believed it," she said.

"I told you I wouldn't be your husband," Jack said. "Sometimes you have to take a man at his word."

"And such a foolish man, too," she said.

Jack counted her teeth. There were plenty of them. "I'm not considered foolish on shore, even if people don't like me much, and I hope I won't be foolish here. Good day."

He turned tail, and swam away as fast as he could without looking like he'd gone into a panic. They were a nasty crowd, those porpoises, and the mermaids weren't much better.

A whistle stopped him in mid-stroke, and he turned to find the fishhook fellow following in his wake.

"Peace," he said. "I've only come to give you a message. We'll support your lawful wife as needed if you'll ally yourself with our clan in any war which might arise in the next ten years."

Jack thought. "I've never been in a war," he said. "I'm not sure if I'd be much use."

"Oh, you'd be useful all right. Mermen. Everyone wants a merman on their side when it comes to teeth and daggers." The porpoise shrugged. "It's mostly just a formality. We haven't had a real war in a long time."

"How long?" Jack asked.

"Maybe nine or ten generations. Somewhere back then there was a true war."

"And do you see any conflicts on the horizon now?" Jack asked.

The porpoise shrugged again, "It's as peaceful a time as any."

"Well then, I suppose we have an agreement."

"Right, so we do. Feel free to visit our clan's waters."

With that, the porpoise swam back to his

clansmen.

§

Jack bobbed to the surface. The sky was turning towards sunset, and in the distance he sighted the familiar flare of the Eddystone Light. He set his course for it. He had the rocks in throwing distance when he heard the now-familiar hiss of a mermaid over his shoulder.

"Jack," said his mother, "what on earth are you thinking?"

Jack swam on without answering.

"I do not think that your father will be pleased," she said as she caught up with him. Jack was happy to see that it cost her some effort to overtake him.

"It is my habit," said Jack, "to pay my respects to Father periodically."

"Hmm." His mother hurried to keep up. "Surely you should pay your respects to *me,* now that you are in my element."

"Had I been given more of a choice, or had you visited me when I was a boy, I might see it that way," Jack said. He slowed down as they reached the edge of the rocks. Even from under the water, they were tricky to navigate.

Jack's mother noticed the box that he was trailing. "Is that for the girls?" she asked. "You should know that mermaids don't like gold."

"No, it isn't," Jack said. "But they don't like gold? What about that one with the gold earrings?"

"Oh, Genevieve?" His mother sniffed. "She's so unlucky that she can't even find enough pearls to make earrings out of. Can you imagine?"

"I can't say that I care much," Jack said. "Besides, I thought her jewelry was quite becoming."

His mother's tail slapped down onto the waves. "Goodness. Then you shouldn't have thrown her back like by-catch then, should you have?"

"That has nothing to do with it," Jack said. "I'm here to see Father. Would you kindly..."

What was it that you asked when you couldn't say, "step out of the way," because the person you were addressing didn't have feet? The question stopped Jack short. He had come with one clear intention: To recapture Iris, with his father's help. He didn't think that his mother's presence would help matters. He was still mulling over the question of how to ask her to go away when the lighthouse door swung open.

"I tell you, there's no one here," said a familiar female voice. "I haven't seen so much as a boat in hours." Aunt Ermie stepped out of the shadow of the lighthouse.

"And who is that?" hissed Jack's mother.

Jack cleared his throat. "Aunt Ermie?" he said. She swiveled around to see him. His mother ducked under the water.

"Jack!" she exclaimed. "Get out of that cold water at once and put on some proper clothing! And what on earth will the barber think of your hair!?"

"Aunt Ermentrude," Jack said, "may I present my mother, Marissa." He reached down until he found her and pulled her up beside him.

"A doxy, if I ever saw one," his aunt muttered.

"A harridan," his mother retorted, shaking the

water from her hair.

Jack's father ambled out of the lighthouse, looking in the opposite direction.

"They're just there now," he said to Aunt Ermie, pointing at the horizon. "The evening boat." He didn't look back at her, or seem to notice her lack of response.

Aunt Ermie ignored him and glared at Jack's mother, who returned her glare with equal venom. They drew closer to one another.

Jack swam around to the dock.

When he emerged there, Jack's father rubbed his eyes. "Goodness gracious, a merman!" he said.

"It's me, father!" Jack said.

Jack's father sat down as if his legs had collapsed. Jack hefted himself half onto the dock. His father's eyes widened with horror.

"My god! Is that...." Jack's father glanced at the approaching rowboat. "Get back down! They'll see you!"

Jack shrugged. "What does it matter to them?"

Jack's father's jaw flapped a moment as he searched for words. "I've never once heard of any of them, let alone myself, seeing a merman, you'd be..."

"You harridan," Jack's mother repeated in the distance. "You told him I was a what?"

"I had no evidence to the contrary," Aunt Ermie sniffed, "and now I see it confirmed with my own eyes."

Jack and his father turned to watch the two females.

"We are a proud race," his mother said.

"Nonsense," Aunt Ermie retorted. "You

wouldn't know pride if it bit you on the nose. Imagine, abandoning a baby at that age!"

"You don't know what it's like!"

Jack and his father looked at each other again.

"So," Jack's father said, "has she married you off yet?"

"She tried to," Jack said, "to about a dozen mermaids, all at once."

"A harem! Ha ha! That's wonderful!" Jack's father said, doubling over with laughter.

"No, it isn't," Jack said. "I promised you I would marry a land girl, and so I will."

"Don't be a fool! When I said not to marry a mermaid, I thought you were going to be a man like me, but now you can swim after those fish-tailed girls any time you like. A harem. Now that will keep you company!" Jack's father grinned from ear to ear. "Tell me, what are they like?" Then he looked over his shoulder at the approaching boat.

"Damnation, they *are* coming this way!" he said. "Hide yourself!"

Jack dove under. The smugglers had never much liked him, even as a human. Now, they might try to take his hide to sell to the likes of Dr. Washington. Jack swam under the surface to a hollow near the dock.

He could hear his father pacing, the clack of Aunt Ermie's heels, and her huffing breath as she climbed back over the rocks.

"Did you tell Jack about the letter?" Aunt Ermie asked.

"No," Jack's father said. "It went clean out of my head. Imagine my son, a merman!"

"I don't think it's anything to be proud of," Aunt

Ermie grumbled.

"So who is this girl?" his father said.

"How should I know?" Aunt Ermie said.

"I know you opened that letter," said his father. "I saw you do it."

In the short silence that followed, Jack heard his mother hissing to herself as if she were plotting something.

"I will say this," Aunt Ermie said at last. "She has a fair hand, a good education at any rate. He could do worse."

Jack's heartbeat quickened. So Iris had written to him. More astoundingly, Aunt Ermie seemed to like what she'd seen.

"But I don't think," Aunt Ermie continued, in a withering tone of voice, "that it's proper for a girl to write to a young man before they're officially engaged, and it seems to have been a *very* brief courtship."

Jack's father grunted. "There's a lady aboard that boat there."

§

The boat's progress must have slowed to a standstill, or else Jack's heart had sped up to an unprecedented rhythm. He heard the oars slip in and out of the water, the creak of them in their pins, and the long breath out as the rowers shipped their oars and took hold of the dock.

"Are you sure you wouldn't rather go on with us to France?" one of the men said. "There's some fine things in France, some fine things."

"Thank you, but no. You see, there's quite a

respectable lady here to act as chaperone."

Jack's father grunted as he helped Iris out of the boat. "We'll keep you safe enough here for the night."

Jack was leaning out towards the edge of his hiding place to hear more when something tugged him abruptly down.

"How did she know you were coming?" his mother demanded, once she had him underwater.

"I only told her to write to me here," Jack burbled. "It was just luck, or maybe the moon."

The moon shone through a break in the clouds on the horizon, orange and full. Jack's mother turned towards it and made an elaborate salutation through the waves. Jack swam back to his hollow and came up for air. Being back at the rocks had stirred up memories of his brothers again. He missed them. When his mother re-emerged, Jack crossed his arms over his chest and squared off across from her.

"Why?" he demanded. "Why did you send me away to be a brotherless orphan, when I could have known them all along, and not just met them again after they'd died?"

"Mermaids so rarely have man-children," his mother said. "When we mate with sailors, or even mermen, it's usually just fish or mermaids, or porpoises and the like."

Over by the dock, the oarsmen were pushing off again.

"You were born to be a merman," Jack's mother said, seizing his hand. "They would have had me butcher one of the others for your tail when you were all just babies, and I couldn't bear it, not even

Georgie, who would never even nurse at my breast."

Jack recoiled. "Would they have?" The mermaids had struck him as frightfully unsentimental, but he wasn't entirely sure that he believed his mother's account of it.

His mother nodded. "I couldn't bear it. They shunned me, you know. The other night, with the mer-king, that was the first time he'd acknowledged me. The girls only spoke to me because they knew that someday I would bring them a merman." Her eyes shifted. Her voice was shaking, as if she wanted to cry, but had no tears to shed. "You've ruined all that."

"I haven't," Jack said. "I'm still a merman."

"I don't know that they'll see it that way."

"They'll have to," Jack said. It didn't matter whether his mother was telling the truth or not, it wouldn't change how he felt about Iris. "Besides, what kind of man can't marry as he chooses, if the girl will have him?"

His mother had no answer to that. She ducked out of the hiding place and looked back at the moon. Jack followed her. The rowers had already covered half the distance to the horizon.

"I suppose you'd better go find out," she said.

Jack swam back to the dock where his father waited.

"The women went inside," he said with a jerk of his thumb. "Here's the letter. I'll go find the girl."

Jack took the letter, but he had to get himself out of the water to open it safely. He took it in his teeth and swam around to a relatively smooth rock a few steps away from the lighthouse.

The lighthouse door opened and Iris emerged alone. She didn't see him at first.

"I'm sorry," Jack said, clearing his throat. "I only just received your letter. I haven't had time to open it, let alone read it."

Iris blinked, then gasped. "My god!" she said. "You're magnificent!"

Jack blushed. "I'm sorry about the letter."

"Never mind that!" Iris said, rushing over to him, and stopping just a few feet away. "It only said that Father tells me to marry whoever I like. He washes his hands of it, as long as he's invited to the wedding and can have a drop of rum before the priest has us say 'I do.'"

"Well, my father hasn't said anything near that," Jack said, "but I've only just gotten here, and... would you really still marry me, even though I can't go on shore? I mean, people might think you were a widow."

"I don't know. I hadn't really thought of it that way, but..." She hesitated.

"What's the trouble?" Jack asked.

"Well, what about those mermaids? Surely one of them might suit you better, now. I mean, unless..."

Jack glanced over his shoulder. He knew that his mother must be somewhere nearby, listening, but he couldn't see her.

"I don't want to marry a mermaid," Jack said, "or even a dozen of them. The whole time I've been in the sea, I've been wanting to get back to you."

"Have you really?"

"I have. It's only been a few days, but I'd go on looking, for as long as it took."

"You would?" Iris said. "But I'm too plain for you, as you are now, I mean."

"You're not," Jack protested. "They wanted me to marry a harem of them, but I don't want to." He started talking quickly, as if the thoughts might get away from him if Iris didn't hear them immediately. "My mother says I was born to be a merman, but I wasn't raised to it. I don't want to give up all I've grown up to be. I don't mind about the accountancy, but I could never be really happy just living in the sea. I need you, to be my link to the land, and also... also just to be you."

Iris blinked back tears. "Really?"

"Really," Jack said.

She came over and sat beside him, with her boots dangling in the water. "You know, I think I need you to be my link to the water, too." Jack took Iris's hand in his, and was about to kiss it when Aunt Ermie stepped out of the lighthouse.

"You need a chaperone, Miss Parker," she said.

"Thank you for your concern, but I'm not really used to having one," Iris said, blushing.

"Humph."

"It's all right, Aunt Ermie," Jack said. "We're engaged."

"Are you now? Then where's her ring?"

Jack's father peeked out, but his eyes focused on something else. "Marissa," he mumbled. Ignoring the young couple, he set off to meet his old lover on the opposite side of the rocks.

"I was just coming to that," Jack said to Iris. "I think there's a ring in here. Maybe we can have it altered to fit?" He pulled the box out of the water beside him and opened it. Both his aunt and Iris gasped. The gold jewelry glistened in the rising moonlight. Iris reached forward as if to feel it, but hesitated with her hand just outside the box.

"Is that all gold?" Aunt Ermie said, peering over Iris's shoulder.

"Mostly," Jack said, "except for a few stones. I don't know what half of them are." He reached in and found the ring he'd noticed the day before. He presented it to Iris. He heard a hiss behind him and saw his father crossing over to meet them. Iris slipped the ring onto her finger. She had to push mightily to get it over the knuckle, but it fit.

"It's beautiful," she said.

Aunt Ermie harrumphed again and looked into the box. "There's enough left over there to buy a house, I'd say."

"Shall we buy a house then?" Jack asked Iris.

"Can you go into a house," Iris asked, "with that amazing tail?"

"I don't think I can, but maybe if we can find one with a boathouse, by the shore some place?"

"Yes," Iris said, "that would be just the thing. Some place where the tides aren't too extreme."

Jack's mother cleared her throat.

"I'm sorry," Jack said. "I should have introduced you. Miss Parker, this is my mother..."

His mother's lips twisted in protest for a moment. "You may call me Marissa," she said. "It's my only name. We don't have that 'Miss' and 'Missus' nonsense among the mermaids. Selkies don't have it either, you know."

"Then you must call me Iris." Iris hesitated. "Would you like me to call you mother?"

Jack's father guffawed. "I don't think that would

be a good idea."

"Marissa will do just fine," Jack's mother said coldly.

And so it was settled. Aunt Ermie escorted Iris back to Plymouth in the morning. They sent word three days later that they'd found a suitable cottage. Jack's father tried to convince Jack to keep the mermaid harem as well as Iris on the shore.

"It would make your mother happy," he said.

"She'll have to find some other way to be happy," Jack said. He went out every day to explore the waters around the rocks. He found shipwrecks everywhere, some with valuables still salvageable in their holds. He sent word of his impending marriage to the mermaid king, via his mother, along with a box of good Cornish pasties, which arrived only slightly damp. His mother returned for the wedding ceremony, looking somewhat mollified. Apparently, she had gained the king's favor, which was perhaps what she'd wanted all along.

Aunt Ermie, in her usual efficient manner, found a priest to conduct the ceremony. Iris's father arrived in time to get the priest so drunk that he wouldn't notice that the groom was up to his waist in water the whole time.

"You know," said Charlie Parker, "I thought my girl would never settle down, and certainly not like this, but if she's happy, well..." he coughed and looked down at Jack's tail. "You know, if you ever want to join the medicine show, a man like you could have 'em coming in from all quarters."

"Thank you for the offer, sir, but I find I like the sea," Jack said.

The priest staggered and slurred his way through the ceremony. At the end, Iris leaped into the water and embraced Jack, kissing him in front of everyone. They stayed there in the water together until long after the guests had gone.

Jack and Iris built a fireplace in their boathouse, and lived there together for many happy years. Iris's father did more and more business in the Plymouth area, and was a frequent and welcome guest at Aunt Ermentrude's house. Jack's father stayed at the lighthouse, but said, with a wink, that he had plenty of visitors now, thanks to Jack's reputation as a romantic among the mermaids.

§§§

The End

THE SONG BEHIND THE STORY:
EDDYSTONE LIGHT

My father was the keeper of the Eddystone Light
Slept with a mermaid one fine night.
From this union there came three,
A porpoise and a porgy and the other was me.

Chorus: Yo, ho, ho, the wind blows free: oh, for the
life of the rolling sea.

One night as I was a-trimmin' of the glin
A-singin' a verse from the evening hymn,
A voice from the starboard shouted, "Ahoy!"
And there was my mother a-sittin' on a buoy.

Yo, ho, ho, the wind blows free: oh, for the life of
the rolling sea.

"What has become of my children three?"
My mother she did ask of me.
"One was exhibited as a talking fish
the other was served on a chafing dish."

Yo, ho, ho, the wind blows free: oh, for the life of
the rolling sea.

Well, the phosphorus flashed in her seaweed hair;
I looked again, and me mother wasn't there.
I heard a voice call out of the night:
"To Hell with the keeper of the Eddystone Light!"

I grew up singing this folk song, usually around a fire on a beach as the sunset faded and stars came out. My extended family, along with occasional friends, had a tradition of gathering for beach picnics several times a summer. We would go down to the beach, collect driftwood for a fire, and cook dinner over it while seagulls circled for scraps. After dinner and s'mores or oatmeal cake, we trotted out a selection of well-worn songs, including this one and several other sea chanteys. We sang them with a combination of loud melody lines, skillful harmonies, and tone-deaf digressions – mostly the later.

Folk ballads don't demand much in the way of vocal skills. It's like an overblown session of singing "Happy Birthday." Participation is more important than perfection. I used to think that these songs had been handed down through the folk tradition, but then I noticed that the vast majority of them had been recorded by Burl Ives and/or The Weavers in the 1940s – 1960s, and that old copies of those records could be found in various family houses. Maybe my parents' generation learned them from professional recordings, but one way or another, they entered our family's repertoire.

I've always liked those songs, especially Eddystone Light with its "rooooooling sea" in the chorus and the slightly ridiculous family relationships. This story is a quick trip into the narrator's life, starting from the night when he meets his mermaid mother.

§

For news and future work, please visit
http://www.ameliasmith.net